Yancy's Luck

On the face of it, Yancy Nodean's mission seemed simple enough: clean up Pine Junction. People were going broke in droves unable to meet the demands of a crooked marshal and three bully-boys called deputies.

Fear cast a long shadow over the town and it looked as if Yancy would never be able to break the hold of those vicious men who ruled the lives of the townsfolk.

But Yancy was one tough hombre with all the gun-skills and determination needed to bring justice to Pine Junction. Soon hot lead began to fly and the hangman's noose was at the ready!

Yancy's Luck

TERRELL L. BOWERS

A Black Horse Western

ROBERT HALE · LONDON

© Terrell L. Bowers 2002
First published in Great Britain 2002

ISBN 0 7090 7044 6

Robert Hale Limited
Clerkenwell House
Clerkenwell Green
London EC1R 0HT

Typeset by
Derek Doyle & Associates, Liverpool.
Printed and bound in Great Britain by
Antony Rowe Limited, Wiltshire

*For the person who makes me believe in
unconditional and eternal love . . .
my darling wife!*

One

Spring was on the way, but there was the chill of winter in the Wyoming air. Konrad Ellington's jacket was open enough for his US Marshal's badge to glint in the afternoon sun. He had been in his share of territorial prisons and they were all pretty much the same.

The guard on the nearest tower watched his movements, curious as to what he was doing walking among the prison population. Konrad surveyed the faces around him. He had some idea of the man he was looking for, but they had never met.

A barrel-chested man, wearing a uniform, carrying a club and sporting a black eye, approached to block his path. 'What's your business, Marshal?' he asked. 'Ain't no one safe in here walking about.'

'I've permission from the warden to round up one of your boys . . . Yancy Nodean.'

The walking boss grunted. 'I hope you're taking his sorry hide to the nearest tree for a hangin'!'

'Not real popular, huh?'

'He give me this eye,' the guard complained. 'Hit me when I wasn't looking.'

'Where's he at now?'

'Got him in cold storage.' He nodded to a corner of the yard, where it appeared there were several cages buried in the ground. 'He ain't goin' to be so tough next go-round.'

Konrad removed a piece of paper from his coat pocket. 'I'm to take him to visit the warden.'

The walking boss tugged his collar against a gust of cold air and looked over the sheet of paper. It was upside down, so it wouldn't have made a difference if it was a legal document or a page from the *Police Gazette*. The head guard obviously couldn't read.

'Looks in order,' he said, passing it back. 'Follow me.'

Konrad fell in behind the man, while he trudged over to the ground cages. As they approached, Konrad might have expected to find a man who was broken in spirit and ready to cry out for mercy. Instead, Yancy had a ground blanket under him, was stretched out on his back, with his hands under his head. He looked about as relaxed as if he was sitting at his favorite fishing hole.

'You got company, Nodean,' the walking boss snorted, lifting up the cage door. 'Haul your carcass out of that there hole and be quick about it.'

Yancy sat up and squinted up at the guard. 'Dag-nab-it, Sweets, I was about to get myself a tan. The sun would have been shining in the hole in another few minutes.'

'You're always the smart mouth, Nodean. I should have taken a whip to you, instead of letting you off with a little time in the hole.'

'That's a nasty-looking eye, Sweets. You run into a door or something?'

The guard was livid. 'Stop calling me Sweets! The name is Kandy . . . with a "K"!'

'If your ma had known you were going to be such a lovable guy, I'll bet she'd have named you Sugar!' With a grin. 'Yep, Sugar Kandy – got a real ring to it, don't it?'

The guard raised his club menacingly. 'I'm warning you, Nodean!'

'Be a good fellow and cut the wise remarks,' Konrad said, stepping forward to look down at Nodean. 'You're going to see the warden.'

Yancy got to his feet and climbed out. Once on his feet, he gave Konrad a curious look. 'What's this all about?'

Konrad was abrupt. 'Close your grub chute and follow me.'

Yancy did as he was told, without any further remarks to the guard. A couple of inmates called or jeered as he passed, but he remained silent and right on Konrad's heels. Once to the gate, a guard allowed them to pass and they crossed a second compound and entered the prison's front building. Konrad led him right to the warden's office and stopped at the door.

'I'm Konrad Ellington,' he introduced himself, 'a United States marshal. I'm expected to keep the peace in Wyoming, Colorado and Montana Territories.'

'I reckon that ought to be enough to keep you busy.'

'I'm empowered to hire deputies and put them where I need them.' He bore into Yancy with his steel-cold blue eyes. 'I sometimes employ a man to do a special job or track down a single killer. It's my law out there, until those territories become states.'

'Where do I fit into this puzzle?'

'I've a job for you, Nodean. It might mean getting yourself killed, but I believe you're the man for the chore.'

'I was sentenced to eight years for killing the Parks brothers.'

'You shouldn't have shot the second one in the back.'

'He tried to get into the dress shop, where he would have grabbed himself a hostage. I hate a guy who hides behind a frightened child or woman.'

'Judge didn't see it your way.'

'I reckon not, what with him being a cousin to the Parks boys. I don't think he was real concerned about the fairness of the verdict.'

'I've got a town with a problem, Nodean. You solve those problems for me and I'll have your record cleared.'

'You want me to go from being behind bars to being behind a badge?'

'Why did you take on the Parks brothers?'

'They ran roughshod over everyone in Center Springs. I watched them beat an old man until he couldn't stand up. I should have ended up the town hero. Instead, I end up going to prison.'

'There's a lesson to be learned there, son. You have better luck if you start out with the law on your side.'

'No argument from me there.'

'How about the walking boss? Why did you poke him in the eye?'

'He was wailing on some new guy with his club. The poor slob would have died, if I hadn't taken a hand.'

'What was this new guy to you?'

'A poor slob.'

Konrad gave a nod. 'You're the man I want for the job. You can take it or spend the next seven years and five months in this hole.'

'Swear me in, Marshal. I'm your man.'

The early spring snow had drifted until it was belly-deep to the team, but they were stout animals. Yancy kept them moving at a steady pace, while watching the rolling black clouds move in to cover the tops of the distant mountains. His mackinaw coat was buttoned up against the chill of the biting wind and his ears were protected by a woollen scarf. With his hat jammed on tightly, it was mostly his feet and hands which were numb from the icy conditions.

The isolated stretch of country was barren and windswept, with the earth covered with the leavings of the three-day snowstorm. All around him, the world was a white vista, an endless void of ice, blowing snow and freezing temperatures. The ivory caps from distant mountains stood like massive icebergs, their heads protruding up from the frigid water, offering no solace, only an added forewarning of danger to man and animal alike.

Pine Junction, Wyoming, was Yancy's destination, still fifty miles up the nearly indistinguishable trail. That meant at least one more night out in the open. He wondered what kind of mess he was getting himself into. Konrad told him there was a job to be done, but he didn't give him much information. His office had received several letters of complaint about extortion, intimidation and unwarranted taxes. It wasn't much to go on.

Removing his gloves, Yancy flexed the cold, icy stubs which resembled his fingers. He stuck one hand at a time into his coat and tucked it under the opposite arm. When the feeling returned, so he could use his hands, he sought his timepiece. There was less than an hour before darkness would cover the land. He began to search the horizon, seeking a place to shelter for the night, perhaps a gully or wash of some kind. . . .

A swirl of wind pelted small crystals of snow into his face. Yancy squinted against the blowing snow and saw what appeared to be a wagon, sitting a short distance from the trail. It was off by itself, covered with a foot of snow. He figured the outfit had probably been abandoned for some time. After all, not many people were foolish enough to travel the plains of Wyoming during the brunt of the winter.

However, there was also a chance the wagon belonged to some ignorant pilgrims, who had been trying to follow the Oregon–California Trail. If so, they might have gotten lost and been broken down for days.

Yancy heaved a sigh of resignation and guided his team in that direction. He had some firewood, grain and food with him. If there was someone with the wagon, they might be in dire need of help.

As he drew closer, his stomach became an empty pit. He swallowed hard and slowed the team to a stop. He could see the wheel was missing on the rear right side of the wagon and the axle had been propped up with a wooden block. More worrisome, beyond the broken-down vehicle, he could see the partially-snow-covered carcass of a horse or oxen. It appeared to have been ravished by coyotes. A second mound, which likely designated another animal, was a short distance away, also covered by an inch-thick crust of snow.

'Hello the wagon!' he called out. 'Is anyone inside?'

Only the howl of the wind answered his query. He set the brake on his wagon and climbed down. Then he went over to the back of the old Conestoga and began to work the back cover loose. It was secured from the inside . . . not a good sign.

With a gloved hand holding the flap, he paused. A nervous traveler might be a little quick to use a gun on an intruder. 'Anyone in there?' he asked loudly once more. 'Sing out, if you can hear me!'

When no answer came, he peeled the canvas door aside and stared into the dark interior. The wagon was loaded with personal belongings and a bed. As his eyes adjusted to the gloom inside the wagon, he inhaled sharply at the sight.

A man was sitting against one of the inner walls, bundled in a heavy coat, with a blanket wrapped about his head and ears. His arms were still crossed for warmth. But there was frost tangled in his thin moustache and on the lashes which were above unseeing, glazed-over eyes. The face was ashen and lifeless; the man was frozen solid.

Yancy uttered a groan of regret and climbed up into

the bed of the wagon. He located a second body . . . a woman. She was under the blankets, but had suffered the same fate as the man. From outward appearances, it appeared she might have been ill. She was emaciated and had been wearing a night-dress. It was likely the man had been tending her when the freezing temperature had taken his life.

Kneeling on the edge of the bed, Yancy knew there was no way he could bury the couple. The ground was covered with a sheet of ice and it was frozen, hard-pack earth underneath. His only option was to try and discover the identification of this couple and gather anything of value. He would load the bodies on his wagon and take them to Pine Junction. From there, he would attempt to notify the dead couple's heirs and ship them anything worth saving. There was not much else he could do.

He crawled deeper into the wagon and found a trunk. He started to open it to begin his search, when a muffled sound reached his ears. It was a soft moan – a human voice!

Yancy swung back around to the bed and quickly tossed the covers aside. Buried below a pile of clothes and blankets, he was amazed to discover a little girl! She was tiny, not more than five or six years of age, curled into a ball for warmth. Bundled in heavy clothing, she was too weak and cold to move, but she was alive!

The next few hours were hectic for Yancy. He quickly threw up a lean-to on the leeward side of the Conestoga and used his own rig to form a second block against the wind. Next, he dug out the dry kindling he had brought with him and started a fire. When it was burning good, he wrapped the child in a heavy blanket and placed her where she could receive the most benefit from the heat. He took a few minutes to rub down his mares and feed them a little grain. Lastly, he tethered them next to the wagon, where they would be protected from the icy chill of the wind.

The little girl was fully conscious by the time he returned to her, but she was still too near-frozen to do more than whimper. He did a quick examination for frostbite and was relieved to discover no ashen or discolored body parts. He was hopeful the cold would leave the child's limbs, but it would not be without pain. He knew that, once the numbing cold started to dissipate, it would be replaced by a throbbing agony. The warming up of near-frozen fingers and toes caused them to feel as if they would explode from pressure. The little girl was going to suffer a great deal.

Yancy started some broth for the child. Before it had time to get warm, her slight body began to shake and she started to cry from the painful warming process. Warming his own hands, Yancy spoke softly to the little girl and began to gently massage her small feet and hands to help promote circulation. She tried to brave it out, but ended up sobbing from the torment. It was a lengthy and agonizing process, but the freeze abated from her limbs after about thirty minutes.

When she had recovered from the chill, Yancy spoon-fed her a little broth and it was enough of a stimulant to bring her appetite to life. He next prepared beans and salt pork for the two of them and the girl displayed a voracious hunger. She ate until he had to take the plate away to prevent her from eating it too.

'I don't want you to get a tummy ache,' he told her. 'If you're still hungry in a little while, I've got some jerky you can chew on.'

She bobbed her head up and down to his suggestion and regarded him with the most sparkling crystal-blue eyes he had ever seen. Her tiny brow wrinkled in a curious frown.

'Who are you?'

'My name is Yancy Nodean. What's yours?'

'Kara . . .' she answered, 'Kara Anders.'

'Where were you and your family going, Kara?'

She lifted her slender shoulders in a shrug. 'Don't know. Daddy didn't have no money. We didn't have nothing to eat and the wagon broke down. It . . . it's so cold.'

He moved over to pull up the heavy quilt and tuck it about her shoulders, before he paused to ask another question. 'Did your folks say you were going to Pine Junction? Do you have any relatives there . . . an uncle or grandparent?'

She frowned in thought. 'Daddy said he was gonna get a job digging coal. He . . .' she cast a fearful look at the wagon, 'he stopped talking. All he did was stare. He . . . he wouldn't talk to me.'

'I know.'

'Mommy's been sleeping for a long time.' She took a deep breath and let it out slowly, with a knowing, yet fearful, grimace. 'Is she ever gonna wake up again?'

Yancy softened his voice as best he could. 'I'm afraid not, Kara.'

Her eyes filled with tears and her lower lip quivered. 'She and Daddy neither?'

He felt his heart swell up until it blocked his throat passage. He was unable to speak the words. He could only nod his head affirmatively.

'Then . . . I don't got nobody.' The tears slid down her cheeks. 'I . . . I don't. . . .' She whimpered each word, 'I want my mommy . . . and . . . and my daddy.'

She began to weep, so Yancy took her into his arms. He held her close to offer what comfort he could. 'There, there, Kara,' he said softly, patting her gently on the back. 'It's going to be all right. You've got to be a big girl.' Than with a bit of reassurance, 'Besides, you're not alone. I'm here. I'll take care of you.'

He wondered at making such a promise to a child. What did he know about raising a little girl? He had not even known his own mother. She had been incapable of handling the strain and duty of motherhood. She had up and deserted her family when he was only a toddler.

Motherless for a dozen years, he had been in his early teens when his own father had gotten stove-up from falling off a horse. After the accident, his father barely scratched out a living doing bookkeeping. Often bedridden with pain, the man had not been able to take care of Yancy. For most of his life, Yancy had been forced to look after his own welfare. Now he had a child clinging to him, trying to be strong, facing the future without her parents. Fate had cast him as her new guardian, but it was a chore he was ill-prepared to handle.

After a few minutes, the small face pulled back to look up at him. Kara sniffed and blinked in an effort to stop the large tears which continued to escape and trickle down her rosy cheeks.

'Will you . . . will you be my new daddy?'

He swallowed against a new constriction in his throat. 'I reckon we had better see if you have some other relatives first. There might be an uncle, aunt or grandparents who will want you to come live with them.'

'I don't 'member having none of those.'

'No cousins you can remember? No one who ever came to visit on Thanksgiving or Christmas for a big dinner?'

She shook her head. 'No.'

'Well, I'll look into it. Once we reach Pine Junction, I'll send out a few wires. I might also find some information in letters, a family Bible or something in the wagon. Soon as we reach town, we'll check and see if we can find some of your kin.'

'What if no one wants me?'

'I'm sure plenty of people would want a pretty little girl like you.'

She frowned. 'But you don't want me?'

'I'd be proud to have you for my own little girl, Kara,' he assured her quickly.

'Then why can't you be my new daddy?'

'You don't even know me, Kara. I've been a freighter and stage driver. I've been in and out of trouble for the past few years. I've done so much traveling and living on my own, I don't know the first thing about being a father.'

'I'm a good girl most times,' she said, quietly. 'I won't be no trouble. I'll do whatever you tell me to do.'

He smiled at her promise. 'Let's not worry about it now. We'll first have a try at finding some of your kin. If we don't, then we'll work out some other arrangement.'

She sniffed and rubbed her nose with the back of her tiny hand. 'I think you'd make a good daddy. You seem nice.'

He put his arm around her. 'I'll be your step-daddy until we get to Pine Junction, Kara. Then we'll find you a proper home. You'll see, everything will be OK.'

Kara put her slender arms around his neck and hugged him. He knew she had no real affection for him as yet. It was an act of desperation. The little girl was all alone in the world and needed to feel someone was still there to care for her. He would be that person – at least, until he could figure out what else to do with her.

TWO

Allyson Jenkins clung to the rope and hurried to keep up. The wind was so strong it kept the folds of her dress pressed tightly between her legs and made it difficult to walk. She ducked her head against the cold and panted from the effort to keep pace with the man on the horse.

'What's with you, Runt?' Curly growled, looking back over his shoulder. 'You move slower than a snail trying to swim upstream! You want for me to let old Thunder here pull you like you were on a travois?'

She used the lead rope from the horse for balance and waded through a snow drift. Even with the horse breaking trail, she had to manoeuvre through a lot of snow.

'I swear, it seems you get slower every time we make the trip into town. You ain't worth a pinch of salt, Runt.'

As was her habit, Allyson ignored Curly's barbs. He badgered her about everything she did, but he had never gotten mean with her. His threats were verbal, not physical.

'Should have left you where I found you,' he continued to complain. 'You'd probably have married some old drunk and be getting fat and sassy by now. I can imagine the sort who would step up and want a saloon swamper as his wife.' He snorted his contempt. 'Yeah, you'd have ended up with some sorry Joe, with a fat beer gut and rotten temper. He'd probably have knocked you around some and kept you pregnant. I'll bet you'd be missing some teeth and have a couple runny-nosed kids by this time.'

Allyson let the man rant on. He liked to talk about how tough her life would have been, had she remained working at the saloon. She had cleaned spittoons, picked up after drunks, washed glasses, mirrors, counters, tables and mopped floors. Ten hours, working seven days a week for her meals and a cot in the storage room. Yes, it had been a rotten life, but she did not consider herself all that fortunate to be with him either. Serving Curly kept her busy from before daylight to well after dark. He not only had her managing the house, doing the cooking, sewing, cleaning and the like, but it fell to her to cut the firewood, tan the hides, skin the animals he brought home and oil and clean his string of traps. For relaxation, she was allowed to curry and tend the horse, shovel out the barn and mend the livestock fences. In return, she was allowed a meager ration of food, a couple of elk hides for a bed on the floor and a blend of rags and animal skins for clothing.

Curly Muldoon was in his fifties, with streaks of white in both his unruly hair and shaggy beard. He had flinty eyes, thick, bushy eyebrows and a leathery face which revealed more wrinkles than a week-old shirt. He had only six good teeth, so he had to mash everything he ate. Even then, he ended up with scraps of food in his beard. A person could have recounted the man's menu for the past week, simply by sorting through the strands of his beard and removing bits of food. If Allyson had dared to taunt him, she would have had a great deal of material for the sport.

Curly was not a bad man, but he was no prize either. He thought first about his own welfare, and treated Allyson as if she were a slave and something less than a human being.

Allyson supposed some of his disdain was because she was not white. Her dark hair and lightly tanned skin was from a Mexican mother. Her father had been white, but she knew little else about him. He had been killed when she was four years old. Her mother and two older brothers had died in the Indian raid. Everyone had been killed but Allyson. Being a child of twelve, she had been offered to anyone who would take her in.

The saloon owner's wife had grown too old and sickly to do the hard work required each day. With no relatives and no one to turn to for help, Allyson had ended up slaving for him for almost four years. Then Curly had won her in a bet and she changed masters.

After two long years of serving Curly and listening to his growling nature, she often wondered if being married to one of the drunks would have been any worse.

The town of Pine Junction rose up in the distance. Allyson hurried her step. She knew Curly's first stop would be the saloon. That suited her fine, as she could stand or sit by the pot-bellied stove and thaw out her nearly-frozen feet. Perhaps, as Curly sometimes did, when wanting to demonstrate his benevolence to the other patrons, he would buy her a hot drink. The bartender there often made treats for kids. He used some chocolate powder, which he mixed into water, then added a bit of cream and a sprinkle of sugar. It was the most delicious concoction Allyson had ever tasted.

They reached town a few minutes later and, in spite of his constant reproach and harsh words, Curly did not disappoint her. Once into the King's Full saloon, he ordered her a cup of the chocolate.

Allyson waited patiently while the man behind the counter stirred up the mixture. She smiled her thanks, when he handed her the cup, then went over and placed it on the pot-belly stove to warm it up. When it was good and hot, she took her drink and moved off to hunker down in a secluded corner of the room.

It was not proper for a decent woman to enter a saloon, but most of the local populace considered Allyson to be a half-breed. She did not count as a woman. Dressed in dirty rags, with wild, stringy hair and hardly more than a sponge bath every two or three weeks, she usually looked the part of an untamed savage.

As she had never spoken a word in public, most people thought of her as a mute or dummy. The notion was fine with her. It afforded her a certain amount of dignity. If she were considered intelligent and normal, she would have suffered shame from her attire or at being inside a saloon. As long as people thought of her as mute and part-Indian, they never gave her presence or looks a second thought.

Curly was in the mood for some fun and games. He sat in at a card game and ordered himself a drink. After the home-made brew he drank at the mountain cabin, regular whiskey did not faze him in the slightest. Allyson had seen him drink a half-quart of hard liquor and never even get red-eyed. He drank to feel good but, as long as she had known him, he had never gotten drunk.

She remembered one time, when he had offered her a taste of his rot-gut. A single sip had caused her to gag and her eyes to water. He'd had himself a good laugh and she had never tried a taste again. She often wondered how the man could have any lining left in his throat or stomach.

Once warm, Allyson removed her buffalo-hide coat and placed it on the floor. She was able to sit down on the garment and lean with her back against the wall. The heat from the stove made her sleepy. Tucking her legs under her, she ducked her head and closed her eyes. She knew Curly would wake her when he wanted to leave.

It seemed Allyson had barely nodded off, when angry shouts awakened her with a start. She blinked her eyes open in time to see Curly standing up, squared-off against a man with a badge.

'You and your boys have your boot-heel on the neck of everyone in Pine Junction, Slone!' Curly snarled the words. 'I'm for thinking it's time you was cut down to size!'

The man he challenged stood erect, a sneer on his lips, eyes as beady and black as those of a snake. Jay Slone had one hand on his gun, poised against Curly. Although Slone was the town marshal, Curly had once told Allyson the man was nothing more than a hired killer. Watching the scene, her heart leapt into her throat. She held her breath, instantly frozen with a gripping terror.

'You come into town like everyone else, you pay the taxes like everyone else,' Slone told Curly. 'That goes for what you sell too. You owe us six dollars for the furs you traded on your last trip.'

'I only got twenty for the whole batch!' Curly growled. 'I'll be a slack-eyed bobcat afore I'll fork over my hard-earned money to the likes of you!'

'It's the law.'

Curly did not carry a gun on his hip. As long as Allyson had been with him, the man used a rifle. He did have a skinning knife, and his hand went to its handle.

'You make your own laws, Slone!' he sneered. 'Well, not this time!'

Slone was not about to take Curly on with a knife. He drew his gun and fired.

Curly grabbed his chest with one hand, while drawing his knife with the other. He managed only a single step forward, for Slone fired twice more.

Horrified, Allyson watched the big mountain man fall. Even before she reached his side, he was dead. Torn between shock and rage over Curly's death, she grabbed up his knife and charged at the man who had killed her guardian.

The sun broke through and warmed the icy crust of
snow. By early afternoon, the temperature was above
freezing. The wagon wheels sank into the drifts and
made it slow going for the team. Yancy kept the team
moving until he finally saw buildings up ahead. He
pointed them out to Kara, who was bundled at his side.

'There's Pine Junction,' he told her. 'We'll get us a
nice hot meal and a warm room for the night. You can
take a bath and sleep in a real bed.'

'Why do I gotta take a bath?'

'When did you have one last?'

She squirmed in her blankets. 'You mean like getting
into a tub and everything?'

'Yeah, a real bath.'

She thought about it for a moment. 'I don't
'member.' Then, with innocent eyes on him, 'When was
your last bath?'

He cleared his throat. 'It's been a few days.'

'Why don't we can take one together?'

That was not a subject Yancy was prepared for. He
awkwardly cleared his throat. 'Yeah, well, it's like I said,'
he was careful to avoid any reply to her suggestion,
'we'll get something to eat and order you up a proper
bath – hot water and all.'

She wasn't going to be put off so easily. 'Don't you
gotta take a bath too?'

'I'll see about it, after we get settled.'

Kara refused to let the subject drop. 'How come I
gotta take a bath and you don't got to?'

'Little girls need to take baths more often than a boy, so she can keep her hair clean and pretty.'

'How often is that?'

'I don't know . . . probably once a month.'

Kara shook her small head. 'That sounds like a lot.'

'We'll figure it out as we go and see how often you need to wash. However, you've got real pretty blonde hair. It's a shame not to show it off.'

'Mama used to brush it for me at nights . . . even when we lived in the wagon.'

'See?' At her reluctant nod, he added: 'With those dazzling blue eyes of yours, you're going to break a lot of boys' hearts when you get older.'

The words brightened her small face. It also revealed several gaps in her smile, as her permanent teeth were beginning to replace the baby teeth.

'Is that fun, breaking boys' hearts?'

'Some girls seem to think so,' he answered. Then he added: 'I don't think you'll be the kind to do it on purpose.'

'Have lots of girls broken your heart?'

'It's been dented a few times, but it'd take someone real special to break my heart.' He grinned down at her. 'Someone like you maybe.'

Kara instantly put forth a serious expression. 'I'd never break your heart. I think you're too nice.'

'I'm glad you think so.'

' 'Sides that, you're my new daddy.'

He laughed. 'For the moment anyway,' he allowed, 'but you'd be surprised how many little girls break their daddys' hearts.'

The wagon rolled up the main street of Pine Junction and gave Yancy his first view of the town. It was larger than he had imagined, with a dozen or more shops, three saloons, a hotel, butcher shop, bakery and a drugstore. A fair number of houses were beyond the main street and there was even a jail, something rare for most towns in Wyoming. In all, his first impression of the town was a favorable one.

'Take a look over there,' he said, pointing to an empty shop, next to a café. 'That little place is for rent or sale.'

'It's pretty small for a house.' Kara was critical. 'It don't have no yard for a dog.'

'It's for a business, not a house,' he replied.

'There's a house!' Kara had located the largest place along the main street. 'That one's got lots of room for a dog and cat!'

Yancy took notice of the massive home. It was two stories high, boasted a big yard and was neatly fenced on all sides.

'I think we'll have to settle for something smaller.' He dampened Kara's enthusiasm. 'If it should end up being the two of us, we won't need so much space. When you get a little older and have to clean the house, you'll be glad to have less rooms.'

'Do I gotta wash clothes and cook too?'

'Not until you're a bit older. You need to go to school and get an education too. Let's not do any planning too far in advance.'

'Yeah, I'm only six,' Kara closed the conversation. 'I'm still a wittle kid.'

He grinned. She sometimes spoke like she was very mature, and at other times it was near baby-talk. He didn't doubt who would run their household – and it was not him! Yancy pulled up in front of the hotel first thing. He got a room for the two of them and ordered a bath to be brought up for Kara. Once she decided taking a bath was not such a bad idea, he left her long enough to look up the local authorities.

The marshal's office was between a general store and a saloon. It looked small from the outside, but it was a deep building. He pushed open the door to discover there were four cells beyond the front office. A man wearing a deputy's badge was sitting behind in a chair, his feet propped up on the desk top, reading the *Police Gazette*.

'The marshal around?' Yancy asked the man.

'He don't work Sundays.'

Yancy had lost count of what day of the week it was. 'I brought in a couple bodies. A man and his wife froze to death about forty miles east of here.'

He looked genuinely concerned. 'That's too bad. Find any money on them?'

'They didn't have a penny to their name. What will it cost to get them buried?'

'About ten bucks each, if you want a box and decent burial. Potter's Field is two dollars and you provide the blankets.'

'Who do I see about the arrangements?'

'We handle it out of this office. There is a local carpenter who makes the coffins for us. Part of the city duties is managing the graveyard.'

Until that moment, Yancy had not seen the shadowy figure in the nearest cell. He paused to take notice. It was a dirty, ragged young woman, and she was scrubbing the floor on her hands and knees.

'Who owns the empty shop up the street?' he asked, getting back to business.

'Hilton Conway, the mayor of Pine Junction. He owns most buildings in town.'

'That must be his house at the end of the street, the big one?'

'You got it.'

'The couple that died had a little girl who survived the cold. I have her over at the hotel. What's the procedure about finding her a home or looking for her next of kin?'

'We ain't got funds for taking in orphans and the like. You can send out some wires at the telegraph office to inquire about her kin. As for a home, that'll be left up to you.'

At Yancy's understanding nod, the man offered, 'There are a number of families around who might take in another kid. You'll just have to ask around.'

'If she don't have any kin, is there any reason I can't keep her as my own?'

'None that I know of. If you want to make it legal, we've a circuit judge due to arrive in a day or two. He can probably have you sign some sort of adoption papers.' He cocked an eyebrow at Yancy. 'You got a wife?'

'Just me and my horses. I never had the time to do much courting.'

The deputy grunted. 'Best find a housekeeper or something then. A single man don't usually adopt kids on his own.'

'Yeah, I'll give it some thought.'

The man got up and pulled his coat down from a rack. 'I'll help you get the bodies into the ice house out back. Reckon we can get them buried tomorrow or the next day. With the ground starting to thaw, we'll be able to dig pretty soon.'

The deputy started for the back of the jail, but stopped at the cell. 'This is laundry day, little rag doll,' he spoke to the ragged girl. 'Soon as you're finished with the floor, you can get started. Remember what Slone told you – you don't work, you don't eat.'

Yancy took a closer inspection of the shabby girl. She appeared to be about twenty, with black hair and dark eyes. She glanced up at both he and the deputy, then gave a nod of her head, before returning to her scrubbing once more.

'Is the young lady there one of the country's desperadoes?' Yancy asked.

'Took a slice out of our marshal with a knife,' the deputy answered, with a tight grin. 'If it had been a couple inches lower, she'd have cut off his head.'

Yancy whistled. 'She must be a holy terror.'

'The marshal killed the man who had looked after her for the past couple years. I guess she was going to even the score. About got the job done.'

'What's going to happen to her?'

'The judge will decide when he gets here. For the time being, she works for her keep. Maybe you ought to think about her for a housekeeper. She never complains . . .' he laughed, 'never says nothing at all, for that matter. The man who took care of her called her Runt and she done his cooking, cleaning and the like. She understands English all right, but she don't talk none.'

Yancy let the matter drop. The town marshal had killed a man, but it might have been a fair fight. He had to wonder, there were a good many towns in Wyoming without any sheriff or marshal. Why did a small place like Pine Junction have several lawmen?

Konrad, he wondered to himself, *what kind of game did you stake me to here?* 'I didn't catch your name. I'm Yancy Nodean.'

'Chaw Benedict,' the deputy responded in return. 'Get your wagon and we'll put those unfortunates into the ice house. I'll need to write up a letter on how they died.'

'I'll bring the wagon around. Is there room to turn around in the alley?'

'A back street runs the length of town. You can circle back to the livery, after we unload the bodies.'

Yancy thanked him and went outside. Water was dripping from the eaves, but it was growing late. Once the sun went down, it would turn cold for the night. He hoped the next day would bring more warm weather. It was late in the month of March, so spring was sure to be close by.

As he drove the team around to the rear of the jail, he dreaded the burial of Kara's parents. It was going to be hard to see her cry over the loss. He knew it would take him some time and effort to put a smile back on her face.

The fact that he had taken such a shine to the little girl was something of a surprise to him. He had never been fond of kids. They had always seemed noisy, constantly fighting or crying about something. They seldom gave a man a moment's peace and were invariably in need of food, comfort or clothing.

But Kara was different. She had called him her new daddy. He had saved her life and was responsible for her. If she had no relatives, he would find a housekeeper and adopt her as his own daughter. The idea instilled a lightness in his chest. His life had definitely taken a new turn. A short while back, he had thought his life was at an end, facing eight years in prison. Now, he had a job which would clear his name . . . so long as he didn't get himself killed. And he couldn't allow that to happen. He had another life to think of besides his own: a small, fragile, beautiful little girl.

Three

Judge Mantie looked over the petition and then put alert eyes on Yancy Nodean. 'Is there a woman in your home, Mr Nodean?' he asked.

'No, Your Honor,' Yancy said. 'But I've been asking around for a daytime housekeeper. Until I find one, I intend to keep the child with me at my place of business.'

That seemed a satisfactory answer. With a noticeable softness to his leathered face, the judge looked at Kara. 'Do you wish to have this man be your guardian, young lady?'

'I sure do,' Kara replied, in a mature-sounding voice. 'He's my new daddy.'

'Then I see no reason to deny this adoption. Deputy Benedict's statement indicates all efforts to find next of kin have failed. As far as I'm concerned, the youngster is an orphan. If there are no objections, Yancy Nodean, I appoint you Kara's legal custodian.'

No one raised their voice to oppose the decision, so he tapped his gavel and smiled at Kara. 'This man is now your father, young lady. I hope you are happy together.'

Yancy did not leave the room, but led Kara over to a chair and sat down. He was curious as to the outcome of the other case on the docket.

'Allyson Jenkins' – Judge Mantie turned to other matters – 'stand before the court.'

The ragged young woman Yancy had seen cleaning the jail cell faced the judge. Her hair was a tangled maze, her clothes obviously unwashed for weeks. She looked like a frightened child – hands clutched together, head ducked slightly, eyes lowered.

'I've had time to study the events leading up to your attack on the marshal of Pine Junction.' He paused to clear his throat. 'It is apparent your actions were motivated by the death of your guardian, Curly Muldoon. An instinctive reaction of man or animal is to strike back, when wounded or cornered. At seeing your caretaker killed by the marshal, I can understand why you attempted to exact revenge for his death.'

The woman showed no outward emotion. She remained standing, poised like a statue. Yancy had learned of the circumstances surrounding the death of Curly.

The judge averted his eyes to Jay Slone. The marshal wore a mask of innocence. Then he looked at Hilton Conway. The mayor was in an expensive, imported suit.

'There have been a number of incidents in Pine Junction this past year which seem to indicate the law is not serving the community, but is working for special interest.' He let the words hang over the room for a few

seconds. 'I am only empowered to make court decisions
as a circuit judge. It is not up to me to pass judgment
about the way a town is run. However, I would remind
those people in authority, that they are employed as
servants of the people and not the other way around.'
He again let the words hang over the room.

Yancy was beginning to understand why Konrad had
sent him. Even the circuit judge thought it strange for
a small town like Pine Junction to have four lawmen.

'In the case before the court,' the judge was speaking
again, 'an act of violence can't go unpunished.' He
reverted his attention to the young woman. 'Allyson
Jenkins, you could have permanently maimed or even
killed an officer of the law in Pine Junction. Therefore,
I am sentencing you to serve sixty days in the local jail
or pay thirty dollars for fines and medical expenses.
Which will it be?'

She offered no reply.

'Do you have thirty dollars?' he tried again.

Allyson turned her head from side to side in a negative response.

'Then you will serve sixty days doing community
service, under the supervision of the marshal's office.
The case is closed. Court stands adjourned.'

Kara tugged at Yancy's sleeve. 'You always make me
take baths. Look at her,' she pointed at Allyson. 'She
needs a bath more'n I ever did.'

Yancy hushed her gently, then started to leave. His
path was blocked by the town marshal. A bandage was
above his ear from where the girl had cut him with a
knife.

'I see you've about moved into the store,' he said.

Yancy nodded. 'I'll be open for business tomorrow.'

'There are a few things you'll need,' Slone told him, carefully. 'I don't know about other towns, but you have to buy a licence to open a business or sell a product inside the city limits.'

'I didn't know about that.'

He lifted his shoulders in a shrug. 'Don't amount to much – five dollars a year.'

'I guess that won't break me.'

'We also have a tax to support improvements and pay for services of the community. We collect the tax at the first of each month.'

Something was beginning to smell. Yancy asked: 'How much is the tax?'

'A flat ten per cent. Any money or barter you take in, the city gets ten per cent.'

Yancy let out a pronounced sigh. 'Ten per cent is pretty steep.'

'Got to pay the bills, Nodean. Can't run a city without a budget to work with.'

'It'll make everything I sell more costly. How are we supposed to get any outside business? No one will come into Pine Junction to spend their money. They'll go someplace less expensive.'

'Nothing else around for fifty miles. The soldiers from Fort Grant don't pay attention to prices. They show up every month with their money burning a hole in their pockets. You'll see, it won't hurt your business any.'

Yancy watched the marshal walk away. Four lawmen,

a licence to sell goods, a tax on everything sold – things were starting to add up. The letters Konrad had received were likely from unhappy shop owners.

'You still looking to find a place to rent for you and the kid?' Chaw Benedict had moved up and was standing next to Kara.

Yancy turned his attention to the deputy. 'We don't need much, but we can't live and eat at the hotel. It's too expensive.'

'The small place behind the bakery is going to be vacant. The couple who lived there couldn't pay the mortgage and are pulling stakes. The bank note runs about six dollars a month.'

'Thanks, Chaw. I'll have a look at the house.'

'It'll be empty by the end of the week,' the deputy replied.

'Yeah, thanks, Chaw,' Yancy said. 'If it looks good, I'll talk to the bank.'

'Hilton Conway has the deed. He owns the bank.'

'The mayor seems to own about everything hereabouts.'

'Pretty much,' Chaw agreed. He turned to leave, but paused to nod in the direction of the marshal. Jay Slone had stopped to glare at the girl, the one who had cut a slice across his temple. Bitter hate showed in his eyes and the set of his teeth.

'Sixty days at the mercy of Slone,' Chaw said. 'That gal is going to wish she had never grabbed hold of that knife.'

'I've taken a look at Slone and his other two deputies, Chaw. You don't fit in with the likes of them.'

'Man's got to have a job, Nodean. Hiring out my gun is the only living I know.'

'Not much of a living, far as I can tell.'

Chaw grinned, shifting a wad of tobacco against his cheek. 'Better than trying to run a business in this town. The taxes will eat you like a starving pack of wolves.'

'Thanks for the tip about the house.'

'Can't say I'm doing you a favor, but you're welcome.'

Yancy took Kara to see the house and discovered a young couple were in the process of loading a wagon with their belongings. When he told the young fellow why he had come, the man looked at him with an odd sympathy.

'You really ought to try another town,' he said. 'This ain't a decent place to live.'

'It doesn't look too bad,' Yancy replied. 'Lot of traffic passing through in the summer months, Fort Grant only a few miles up the road, and I see we have one of those coal mines nearby.'

'You'll find out we pay a high price for that coal, mister. Until the railroad runs a spur this direction, the only way to move the stuff is by wagon. The expense to haul it costs more than the market will pay.'

'I never thought about it.'

'Yep. It's sixty miles to the nearest railroad dock. By the time men and teams transport the stuff in freight wagons, there isn't any profit. They need the railroad to lay track this direction so the coal can be shipped right from the mine.'

'You seem to know something about the process.'

'I worked at the mine for a time.' He grunted in disgust. 'Did you know there was a tax on wages here in Pine Junction?'

Yancy frowned. 'I was told that I had to pay a tax on anything I sold or any money I took in for my work.'

'Yeah, well, if you hire an employee, you have to pay ten per cent tax on his wages to the city government.'

'Who is the city government?'

The man laughed without humor. 'Mayor Hilton Conway is the government. He owns Marshal Slone and the three deputies. They do his collecting. Me and the wife are fed up with it. By the time you pay taxes on your wages, taxes on what you sell, then pay taxes on anything you buy here, there isn't any money left to live on.'

'Sounds like we need a new form of city government.'

'Run against Conway for election and you'll end up with your name printed on a cross at the graveyard,' the young man warned. 'This town is under the man's thumb. He has the guns to back him up, the law on his side and he and his wife are friends of the territorial governor. Try bucking that kind of power and you'll end up losing every time.'

Yancy began to see why Konrad wanted a deputy to investigate Pine Junction. The problem was, what did the man expect him to do? How could he take on a half-dozen men by himself?

Setting aside the man's warning, Yancy and Kara looked over the small house. It had two rooms and a small backyard. It would be enough for her to play in and there was ample space to keep a pet. Until she got to know some of the other kids for playmates, Yancy would have to entertain her with a couple of toys and try to get her a dog or cat for company. He decided to ask around for a pet, once he got his shop opened.

'Is that going to be our house?' Kara asked, when they returned to the main street.

'Do you like it?'

'It has real windows,' she said. 'Our last house had paper pasted over the holes and a dirt floor. It only had one room too.'

'Think it'll do us?'

She smiled up at him. 'Sure, Daddy. I like it a lot.'

Something about her calling him *daddy* made his chest inflate. He had hold of her hand and turned toward the general store.

'Now that you are legally mine, I think it's time to get you a new dress and shoes. Maybe we can find something else at the store.'

'I had a baby once,' Kara told him wistfully. 'She had button eyes and some red-colored yarn for hair. I called her Mary.'

'What happened to her?'

'I left her outside and the neighbor's dog chewed her face off' Kara let out a big sigh. 'Guess I wasn't a very good mommy.'

'Accidents happen.'

'Think I'll ever get another doll?' There was a crafty twinkle showing in her eyes.

'We'll see,' he said, knowing that Kara was already working on wrapping him around her little finger. For some reason, he didn't mind one little bit.

*

Hilton stood at the second-story window and surveyed his town. The snow was melting rapidly. He hoped it was the last of the winter season. The freight wagons had been idle for too long. He had to start shipping coal to the railroad and get back into business.

Flora was busy entertaining downstairs. She enjoyed being the queen of Pine Junction. She was happiest arranging parties or hosting a dance or special dinner. With the warmer weather, she could again look forward to a number of trips to Cheyenne or Denver to enjoy the bright lights, fancy gowns and important people of high society.

Thinking of the beautiful woman, Hilton gazed at his own reflection in the window pane. She was twenty-four years old, strikingly attractive, with golden hair and an unblemished, ivory complexion. He was nearing fifty, and self-conscious about the loss of his hair that displayed a large bald spot.

There were no false conceptions in his relationship with Flora. She served as his wife, and he gave her everything in the world she asked for. It had taken everything he had to win such a prize.

She, in turn, had been searching for financial security when she met him. She wanted to be royalty, the queen of an empire. Selecting Hilton had been only after weighing all of her options. She had married him for his money and ambition. No excuses or false pretensions; each of them wanted what the other had to offer.

Below him, up the street, Jay Slone came out of his office. The woman prisoner followed him obediently. He pointed up and down the walk, speaking to her. Then he went to the side of the building and produced a shovel.

As Hilton continued to watch, the slight woman began to clear the walks of snow. It was a heavy mixture of slush and mud. He could see her strain to scoop each full shovel. Knowing Slone's vengeance, he expected the young woman would be working until dark. Slone was a proud, arrogant man, and she had cut him with a skinning knife. He would garnish a mountain of dividends from her attack.

A wagon and team started up the main street. He turned his attention to the young couple atop the wagon seat. The baker and his wife were leaving town. That would be a loss, for they had made wonderful bread and pastries.

He felt a pang of regret. It was his doing that had forced them to leave Pine Junction. The baker had continually spoken up against the city taxes and complained openly about the coal mine bankrupting every business in town. In his effort to sell his merchandise at a reasonable price, he had gone broke. Without the exorbitant taxes, he might still be in business.

Hilton suppressed the twinge of guilt. He would do whatever was necessary to make Flora happy. He needed the income to supplement the mine and fund his own expenses. His wife needed a house servant, fancy gowns and jewelry. She had to travel in luxury and stay at the finest hotels when they were on holiday.

If he failed to satisfy her hunger for such things, she might pack up and leave him. He couldn't bear that.

'Excuse me, Sir?' a familiar voice came from behind him.

'Yes, Jarvis?' Hilton replied, turning to face his butler.

'The luncheon shall be served in a few minutes. I thought you might wish to dress, as Mrs Conway has guests.'

'Did the judge come?'

'He declined the invitation . . . as usual.'

Hilton nodded. 'I'll be along shortly. Thank you, Jarvis.'

The butler wore traditional English servant attire. He had been an out-of-work tailor when Hilton found him. He was educated, but arthritis had taken the dexterity from his fingers. He could not use a needle for more than a few minutes without a lot of pain. He kept to himself and served the Conways very well as a butler.

With a last glance at the departing baker and his wife, Hilton let out a pronounced sigh. He would miss the fine pastry in the future. Perhaps another baker would come to Pine Junction, one who was willing to make the best of the arrangement.

He turned to his closet and selected a dinner jacket. He would comb his hair forward to cover the baldness and don a fashionable string tie. He would let his wife entertain the guests, while he sat back and drank in her youthful beauty.

*

Yancy unloaded the last of his goods and arranged the items for show. Konrad had given him an open voucher for his tools and supplies and a hundred dollars for expense money. It offered Yancy a chance to start a new life. Once his job was finished, the inventory was his to keep. On display were six saddles, some bridles, spurs and a dozen pairs of boots. During his years of roaming from one job to another, Yancy had worked for a boot and saddle maker. He had learned the trade, but was too footloose to stay in one spot. He had never thought he might one day end up with his own store.

He had the forms and tools to make boots and saddles, plus he had an adequate supply of rawhide and leather. To complete his inventory, he had a variety of hats, neckerchiefs and slickers.

'What are these?' Kara asked, holding up a decorative piece of metal.

'They're called cheeks. Those fit on either side of the bit that goes into the mouth of the horse.'

She laughed. 'Cheeks? Like my cheeks?'

'Sure.' He smiled at her. 'A horse doesn't have them.' At her curious frown, he continued. 'That's why we put them on a bridle, so the horse can have cheeks.'

Kara laughed at the explanation and picked up a pair of spurs. She spun the rowel and continued her line of questions. It seemed that was one thing she never ran out of . . . more questions.

Even as he answered her patiently, his attention was averted to the walk. The ragged prisoner he had seen in court was shovelling the porches along the street. She appeared little bigger than the shovel in her hands. She paused, after several scoops, to catch her breath, and the marshal came up from behind and gave her a swift kick to her backside.

'No one told you to stop working, Runt!' He heard the lawman's gruff words. The young woman angrily spun on him with the shovel raised to retaliate. Slone was too quick for her. His one hand flashed out and caught hold of the shovel handle and the other grabbed a handful of her jacket. Then he lifted and twisted her around, giving her a hefty toss with the same motion. She sailed off of the walk and sprawled into the sloppy street. Quickly, she got up on to her hands and knees.

The marshal laughed at her. 'Teach you to attack me, you little half-breed witch! Root in the mud like the swine that sired you!'

The young woman slowly picked herself up, shook the mud and water from her hands, then picked up the shovel and made her way back to the wooden walk. She glared at the marshal, but began scooping off the walks once more.

'I want you to watch the store, Kara,' Yancy told his daughter. 'We are still closed, so no one should come in.'

'OK, Daddy. I'll keep watch for you.'

'I'll be back as soon as I can.'

Kara smiled. 'I'll sweep the floor while you're gone.'

'What a good girl you are.'

That broadened her semi-toothless grin. He leaned

down and kissed her on the forehead, then grabbed up his jacket and hat.

He had something to do. It might not be the smartest trick he could pull, but his conscience would not let him stand by any longer. He was going to make Pine Junction his and Kara's home. It had to be a place he could live in with his head held high.

Four

The sun had set, but there was no let-up in Jay Slone. He kept watch over Allyson and forced her to work steadily. She had slowed down considerably, barely able to lift each scoop of snow. The temperature dropped with the setting of the sun. The puddles and slush would soon be crusted over with ice.

Yancy stepped over in front of Allyson and blocked her path. She paused and put curious eyes on him. 'I believe you've finished for the day, Miss Jenkins,' he told her.

Slone strode down the porch to confront Yancy with an angry glare. 'What's the idea, Nodean? You trying to make up the rules for my prisoner?'

'Not at all, Marshal,' He spoke the words evenly, while forking over a sheet of paper to Slone. 'I'm taking custody of my charge.'

The marshal looked at the paper and then frowned. 'What does this mean?'

'It means that I paid the young woman's fine. The remainder of her sixty days servitude is payable to me.'

48

'What?' Slone was livid. 'You can't do that!'

'I need someone to help look after my little girl. I decided to use Miss Jenkins, until I find someone else for the job. She'll be able to help maintain my shop as well.'

'You must be touched in the head, Nodean! You're going to let this half-breed savage stay under the same roof with you?' He laughed at the idea. 'She'll cut your heart out in the night and light out of the country.'

'I guess I'll have to take that chance.'

Stone sobered, turning his hot gaze on the girl. 'We ain't even yet, dirtbag. One day soon, I'll pay you back for cutting me up. You hear me, Runt?'

Yancy waited until the marshal stomped away. Then he displayed a smile as a peace offering. 'I imagine this is a little confusing to you. Do you understand what is going on?'

She gave her head a negative shake.

'Judge Mantie is still in town, awaiting the next stage, so I went to him and paid your fine. Instead of you staying in jail and being forced to work for the town marshal, you are now in my custody. That means you work for me until your fine is paid back.'

She was still puzzled, as Yancy took the shovel from her and propped it against the wall of the nearest building. 'Come on. Let's get you warm and cleaned up.'

He led the way and she followed like a well-trained animal. No questions, no objections, no outward emotion. She was very much like an Indian squaw, used to doing what she was told.

'Gee, Daddy, she's awful dirty,' Kara said, upon

seeing what Yancy had brought back to their shop.

'You can help her, Kara. I want you to take Allyson to the house and help her start some water to heating for a bath. I'll go over to the general store and pick out something for her to wear. Can you handle that all right?'

'Sure, I can,' Kara replied. 'I'll show her how to take a bath.'

'Good girl.' He spoke to Kara. When he turned his attention to Allyson, she was openly bewildered. 'Miss Jenkins, you go with Kara. As I told you before, you have a legal obligation to work for me until your debt is paid. Do you understand?'

She hesitated, then gave an affirmative bob of her head.

Yancy let the two of them out of the store and locked it for the night. Then he hurried over to the general store and picked out some clothes for his indentured worker. When he came out of the shop, a man with shaggy black hair was waiting for him.

'I'm Zip Lovendaul,' the man introduced himself. 'I'm a deputy marshal here in Pine Junction, Mr Nodean. I'd like a word with you.'

Yancy had the bundle from the store under one arm. He shifted it to a different position and waited. When the deputy's fist shot out, he was caught totally unprepared. The punch hit him flush along the side of the jaw. It was hard enough that he staggered back against the wall of the general store. He dropped the package as Lovendaul unleashed a violent attack.

A shot to the eye blinded him. He felt the wind

knocked from his lungs from another blow. Then he was sitting on the porch, dazed, tasting blood from where his teeth had cut the inside of his mouth.

'There's a lesson for you, Nodean,' the deputy sneered. 'Don't go getting cute behind the marshal's back. You pull another stunt like today, I'll be back to finish this.'

Yancy found his senses returning. He was still unsteady from such a savage attack, but his head cleared. He rose slowly to his feet, spat a mouthful of blood into the snow and watched the deputy swagger off down the street. He was not hurt, only battered some. It was a warning to not cross Slone again. Yancy fought to suppress his anger.

'Your time is coming, pard,' he avowed. 'Cast a big shadow while you can.'

However, he knew better than to go after the deputy and start anything yet. First, he had to figure out how to break the mayor's stranglehold on Pine Junction. Plus, there were four lawmen in town. To tackle Lovendaul might be to end up getting himself killed. He had to put aside his impulse and manly pride. The line had been drawn in the dirt. To step over it would be to start a fight for which he was not yet ready.

'Stay the course and bide your time,' he told himself aloud. Even as the words were spoken, he felt the resurgence of rage boiling within him. He had never before taken a beating without putting up a fight. The deputy had caught him by surprise and he'd not had a chance this round. When the rematch came, he would not be caught unawares.

*

'Daddy said you got to take a bath,' Kara was steadfast. 'You got to do it right.'

Allyson looked down at the little tyrant. Kara had her hands on her hips, poised as if ready to take her on physically.

Kara continued, as if rationalizing the situation. 'Daddy makes me get in the tub and wash from tip to top. If I got to, you got to.'

Allyson surveyed the room, but it was completely open. There was no privacy, no way to safely take a bath. Regardless of what Kara wanted, she was not about to be caught in the middle of a bath, when the girl's father returned.

'What's the matter with you?' Kara kept after her. 'You're real dirty. Daddy says girls have got to wash. They got to be clean and pretty, so they can break boys' hearts. Don't you want to break boys' hearts?'

Allyson had to smile at the logic. 'I suppose so.'

'Well, then, what'cha waiting for?'

'I can't take a bath out here in the open,' she finally explained to the child.

A light shone in Kara's eyes. 'Oh! You need to be in privacy.'

She enjoyed the girl's use of language. 'Yes. I need to be in privacy.'

Kara pointed to the corner. 'Daddy hangs a blanket up for me. How about that? You can hang a blanket, cause you got long arms. I can't reach.'

'All right,' she gave in at last.

The tub was situated in the corner and, true to Kara's word, there were several hooks in the ceiling for attaching the blanket. Allyson was able to drape off the enclosure to make the area into a private little room. Kara showed her where the soap and towels were and even helped fill the tub with hot water. Then she watched Allyson expectantly. 'I'd like to take my bath alone.'

Kara was agreeable. 'OK, if that's what you want. Just be sure to get clean. Daddy always looks behind my ears and everything.'

'I'll do a good job,' she promised.

'I'll put wood in the stove so the fire stays hot. That way you won't catch cold.'

'That's very thoughtful of you, Kara.'

The little girl parted the blankets and hurried to add fuel to the pot-bellied stove. Allyson took a deep breath and began to strip off her heavily soiled rags. She quickly eased into the tub, hoping to be finished before the man returned to the house.

Settling down was a tight squeeze, but she was able to sit with her knees up and the water came almost to her shoulders. The relief of getting the dirt off was secondary to the heat of the water relieving the ache in her bones. Her muscles were stiff and sore from working so hard with the shovel. She winced at the blisters on her hands, which burned from the water. Jay had not let up for a minute all day. Each time she stopped, he had poked or kicked her.

As she began to scrub, she wondered about the stranger. She had no idea who he was. However, she had been at court when he adopted the little waif, Kara.

He seemed to have a good heart – on the surface. As for him paying her fine, she had no idea why he would risk provoking Jay Slone on her account. It was a very dangerous thing to do.

Allyson didn't dare enjoy the luxury of the bath for too long. She quickly washed the dirt and grime from her arms and face, then climbed out of the tub. After she wrapped the towel about her, she got down on her knees, ducked her head over the tub rim and washed her hair. It had been weeks since she had managed to use soap and water to do a decent job of bathing.

The door opened to the house. She felt the instant rush of cold air. Her heart stopped. A wave of panic swept over her. She held her breath and stared at the flimsy blanket petition. At any second, she feared the man might stride over and sweep them aside to invade her privacy!

'Hi, Daddy!' Kara was all smiles. 'I'm watching the fire so Allie can stay warm.'

'Good girl. I'll fix us something to eat.'

'What happened to your eye?'

'I bumped into the door at the store,' he said, telling her a little white lie. 'Someone was coming in when I was going out.'

'Did it hurt?'

'Some, but I didn't cry. I'm all grown up, you know.'

'What's in the package?'

'It's for our guest. You give it to her, while I start supper.'

Kara took the package and headed over to the blanket petition. Yancy went to the cupboards and removed the makings for beans and salt pork. He had some left-over cornbread, so that would have to make the meal.

'Is Allie staying with us?'

'How come you call her Allie?'

'She don't care. It's easier to say than Ally-lay-son.'

'It's Allyson.'

'I know,' Kara quipped. 'But Allie is still more easy to say.'

Yancy shook his head. 'I think the school teacher will have her hands full with you. *More easy?* – you have a problem with grammar, daughter dear.'

'That's OK, cause I don't count none either yet.'

He smiled down at her. What a joy she was. He could only imagine what her real father and mother had been like. He hoped, wherever they were, they knew she was being loved and cared for.

The pork began to sizzle and the beans were hot by the time Allyson appeared from behind the wall of blankets. Yancy glanced in her direction and then stopped to stare. A wondrous transformation had taken place. The ragged, half-animal was no longer in his house. Attired in the pink and white cotton dress, Allyson had a demure flush to her cheeks. Her ink-black hair was damp, yet it decorated her face like a costly frame would house a beautiful picture. *Beautiful*: it was a word which stuck in his mind. Dark eyes, petite nose, sensuous lips . . . yeah, beautiful was the right word.

'Ah-h . . . there's a brush next to the bed in the other room.' He finally regained control of his voice. 'I reckon Kara won't mind if you use it to get the tangles out of your hair.'

'You bet!' she was enthusiastic. 'I'll get it for you, Allie.'

Yancy turned back to his cooking, while keeping watch over his new guest out of the corner of his eye. She went to the single mirror hanging on the wall and began to comb out her wet hair. He noticed how she paused at her own reflection, looking up and down at herself, as if to take a physical inventory. He could only guess what she was thinking. He wondered how long it had been since she had dressed like a normal girl.

'I didn't want to buy you shoes that wouldn't fit,' he spoke over his shoulder. 'Tomorrow morning, we'll go over to the store and pick up some stockings and shoes. You can also get whatever personal items you need.' He paused, 'Unless you have those things at your old house?'

Allyson rotated enough to look at him. He felt her dark-eyed scrutiny, but kept his attention on the nearly-ready pork.

'The marshal took everything Curly owned . . . to pay for back taxes.' She shrugged her slight shoulders. 'Besides, I was wearing most everything Curly ever gave me.'

He smiled, relieved she could talk and enjoying the sound of her voice. 'Like I told you first off, I need someone to help with Kara and the store. You can do the kitchen chores and give me a hand tending to the store. Once you have put in the remainder of your sixty days, you'll be free to make your own choices.'

'See, Daddy?' Kara jumped into the middle of the conversation. 'We got a whole family now. You're my daddy and Allie can be my mommy!'

Yancy about spilled the pan he was holding. He was forced to clear his throat before he could speak. 'The lady is only staying with us for a few weeks, Kara. I don't think you ought to start calling her mommy.'

She didn't notice his unease. 'OK, but me and Allie is gonna be friends.'

'Good. You can be a big help to her around the store and the house, until she learns where everything is at.'

'What's your name?' Allyson asked him.

'Yancy Nodean.'

'Mr Nodean, you are making a dangerous enemy because of me. I'm not worth the trouble you will cause yourself.'

He twisted to put a hard stare on her. 'What makes you think you're not worth a little trouble?'

She lowered her eyes and stared at her bare feet. 'I'm only half-white and was raised by a saloon owner for several years. With Curly, I was a personal slave. I can only read or write a few words and everyone in town thinks I'm half-Indian and can't talk.' When he offered no comment, she spoke again.

'Besides that, I don't know how to behave like no lady. Curly Muldoon was an uncivilized mountain man, and I kept his home for two years. I'm sure most people think he . . . that he and I were. . . .' She swallowed hard and glanced at Kara. 'Well, you know what they think.'

'Not to worry, Miss Jenkins. My little Kara will instruct you on becoming a lady.' He grinned. 'As for the gossip, I've got a thick hide. You need a place to stay and I need someone to look after my daughter. We'll have to both make do.'

'Don't think I'm not grateful, it's only—'

'Dinner is ready,' he cut her argument short. 'Come and sit down at the table.'

Allyson and Kara spent the morning getting the small house in order. A second bed was added to make room for the new live-in guest. Yancy allowed the girls to have the bedroom, where they shared the larger bed. For himself, a cot was placed along one wall in the main room.

The store opening was quite an event. Everyone in town wandered through to see what Yancy was offering. His Ellenburg saddle and embroidered boots drew most of the attention. As the day progressed he took in several orders and sold a few small items.

Late that afternoon, Allyson was washing his storefront window and Kara was sweeping the floor. He was busy making entries in his daily sales book when Hilton and Flora Conway arrived at the door.

Flora swept the room with a cool speculation. When she spotted the saddles, she strode smoothly into the shop. She ran her hand over the leather and remarked: 'Hilly, look at the fine craftsmanship of this saddle.'

'Very nice,' Hilton replied. 'It appears we have a respectable leather shop in Pine Junction. That should please some of the nearby ranchers and soldiers from the fort.'

The woman put scintillating green eyes on Yancy.

She was decked out in a lush fur shawl, yellow satin gown and sported a parasol over one shoulder. Her golden hair was perfectly curled into a French twist at the back of her head, with locks of silken hair showing beneath her stylish derby hat. When she smiled, Yancy felt his knees grow weak.

'I'm Mrs Conway,' she introduced herself. 'Welcome to Pine Junction, Mr Nodean.' Her eyes flicked towards Kara. 'Welcome to you and your little girl.'

Yancy did a slight bow. 'Thank you, ma'am. It's a real pleasure to meet you.'

'I'm afraid I shan't be shopping with you often, Mr Nodean,' she apologized, with a slender simper on her lips. 'Your inventory doesn't hold much interest for a lady. I don't wear cowboy boots or chaps,' she laughed politely. 'However, I have, on occasion, wished to ride a horse. Are you familiar with the English saddles for ladies?'

'I've never actually constructed a side-saddle, but I have seen a couple back east. I could probably build up a form and make one.'

'Excellent. When could you have it ready?'

He paused and took a long look at her, trying not to stare, yet wanting to gauge her size and approximate weight.

'You have a question?' she asked, wondering at his lengthy pause.

'I usually measure a rider for a fit,' he replied.

She laughed at his explanation. 'I'm an inch over five feet in height and weigh about one hundred pounds.'

'Thank you, ma'am.'

'I prefer darker colors – mahogany is nice – for the saddle. It will go fabulously with my favorite riding horse, Goldy. She's a Palomino. Hilly gave her to me for my birthday, but I seldom ride her because I loathe to ride astride.'

'I'll use treated leather and tan it dark. Do you prefer gold or silver trim?'

'Silver, I'm sure. Gold would clash with the color of my horse.'

'I can probably have the saddle ready in a week to ten days.'

'That will do nicely,' she said. Then she tipped her head ever so slightly. 'Good day to you, Mr Nodean. Welcome again to Pine Junction.'

Hilton didn't ask about the price of the saddle, but instead, opened the door for her and followed her out. He hurried to take her arm, escorting her along the walk.

Allyson was at the window to watch them. Yancy could see the envy in her gaze.

'Gee, she's pretty,' Kara stated. 'Bet there ain't a more pretty dress anywhere than the one she's got on.'

'Clothes don't make the woman, Kara.' He winked at her. 'And I think you are a whole lot prettier than she is.'

Kara giggled.

Yancy was about to close for the day, when three men came into the shop. One owned the general store and the other two also had businesses in Pine Junction.

'Howdy,' he greeted. 'Come on in.'

The three stopped well inside the store. One of them

kept watch out of the window, while the other two confronted Yancy.

'I'm John Tompkins,' the store owner spoke up. 'We met at my mercantile.'

At Yancy's nod, he went on with the introductions. 'The man at the window is Calvin Smith. He owns the tavern at the edge of town. This other gent is Everett Wade, owner of the High Card Saloon. We represent the independent businessmen in Pine Junction – those being the stores or properties that are not owned by Hilton Conway.'

Yancy wondered what the three wanted with him. He shook the hands of the two men and gave a tip of his head to the third. 'What can I do for you fellows?'

'It's what we are trying to do, Nodean. That's why we're here.'

'All right, I'm listening.'

'You know about the licence fee and the taxes in this town?'

He sighed. 'Yeah, the marshal was good enough to point out the benefits of joining your fair community. Ten per cent tax and I have to buy a licence each year.'

'That's only the beginning,' John said. 'It gets much worse.'

'And do you know where all the tax money goes?' Wade asked.

'Not right off.'

'It goes to support that coal mine. Hilton is trying to get enough money together to build a railroad spur from here to Cheyenne. It would allow him to ship his coal by rail car. He thinks he'll one day make a fortune with his coal.'

'Wouldn't that also suit the town's purpose?' Yancy tried to be objective. 'After all, a railroad spur would add travelers and customers for the rest of us.'

'You know how much money the spur will cost? It's going to break all of us.'

'Ten per cent tax hurts, but it won't break us.'

John hissed his words. 'That's this year! There's talk of raising it to fifteen per cent this summer. If Hilton can't make enough money that way, he'll up it to twenty!'

'The man is going to strangle us all,' Calvin put in from his place by the window.

Yancy suspected one or more of these men had sent letters to Konrad. He kept it in the back of his mind, while playing dumb. 'What can be done? How do we fight an increase in taxes?'

'All we have to do is get Hilton out of power. We vote him out of office.'

Yancy did some quick thinking. His job was to solve the problems in Pine Junction. He had thought to try and arrest Hilton for fraud, but maybe there was an easier way. 'You think that'll happen?'

'The election is next month. We have to act now or we'll all go broke.'

'What's your plan?' Yancy wanted to know.

'We run our own candidate against Hilton, someone the people will support. When Hilton loses the election, the marshal and the others can be fired and most of the taxes abolished. We keep just enough to pay for what city government we really need.'

Yancy uttered a low whistle. 'I don't think I'd want

the job of getting rid of the four tough men wearing badges. How would you fire them?'

John kept his voice down, as if afraid he would be overheard. 'We've done a little checking . . . real care-ful-like. The judge will oversee the elction and the army has agreed to supply us with a small contingent of men to keep the peace.'

'OK, so what's your plan?'

'Calvin is going to run against Hilton. When we elect him to office, he'll appoint another man as marshal and the army will see that the four lawmen turn in their badges and leave town peacefully.'

'What do you want from me?'

'You will be eligible to vote. We want you to support Calvin.'

Yancy looked at the three men. He read something they still weren't telling him. 'You can count on that. What else?'

'When Slone or Hilton hears of what we're up to, there will trouble. We need the support of every able man to stand up against their gunmen.'

'I won't hide the fact I support your man.'

There was a short silence, then Calvin looked at John expectantly. 'Go ahead, ask him.'

'Ask me what?' Yancy felt a wave of new suspicions.

John cleared his throat. 'We haven't selected anyone for the job of marshal, Nodean. I believe you used to be a freighter.'

'So?'

'Most men who haul freight are fair shots with a gun and know how to handle themselves in a fight.'

'So are most men who run saloons.' He directed the reply at Wade.

'It so happens that Everett did offer to take the job, but he broke his hand a couple years back and can't use a handgun. We would prefer to have an able-bodied sort with the kind of backbone you've shown.'

'Me?'

John grinned. 'It took some nerve to go over Slone's head and take that 'breed out from under his nose.'

'The lady doesn't answer to the title of breed,' Yancy informed John tightly.

The ire in Yancy's tone of voice only widened his grin. 'See what I mean? You've got the guts to back up your notions. I knew that would get a rise out of you.' He turned to look at Allyson. 'I apologize for the vulgar term, Miss Jenkins.'

'What do you say?' Calvin asked. 'We need someone like you.'

Yancy considered the idea. He was already a deputy US marshal, but he couldn't come out in the open yet. To accept just a job might compromise his authority for doing an independent investigation.

'I'm sorry, fellows, but I barely got my foot in the door here. I haven't fired a gun in several months and I sure don't want to test my skill against the likes of Jay Slone. I think you ought to try and get someone else.'

John let out a deep sigh. 'All right, Nodean. We expected how, you being new to town and all, you would probably turn us down.'

'I'll help where I can, but I'm not the man for the job of town marshal.'

'We look forward to what support you can give,' John said. 'Thanks for your time, Nodean.'

'Anytime.'

The three men left and Yancy locked the door behind them. He pulled a curtain across the single window, throwing the room into near-darkness.

'Sounds like this town is heading for a storm,' he observed.

'They can't stand up to Hilton and the gunmen,' Allyson said, quietly. 'Curly stood up to Slone and was shot down in cold blood. Anyone who pits themselves against that group will end up dead.'

'Take a US marshal to take on these boys,' he said prudently. 'I hope the decent men who just left are real careful.'

Five

Allyson stared at the dark ceiling, as she waited for sleep to overtake her consciousness. She was careful not to move around, as she didn't wish to wake Kara. Rolling her head to one side, she could see the tiny form, curled up with her doll in her arms. She was a precious little girl.

Studying Kara caused her to also think about the man in the next room. It had been eleven days since Yancy had paid her fine and rescued her from the brutal marshal. Her mind sifted through what she had learned of him. He was only average in looks, but there was a kindness in his manner and a gentleness in his eyes. He enjoyed smiling and constantly kept Kara entertained. He was broad of shoulders and had strength and confidence in his make-up.

As for Kara, the little girl was as sweet as a candy stick. She loved to be held close, loved to tease and play games and loved to do things to please Yancy. She had accepted Allyson without question and they got along famously together.

It was an odd twist of fate that had put Allyson in a stranger's house. Kara was asleep, but she could hear Yancy moving about on the other side of the curtains. He often worked late into the night to finish projects for customers.

She remembered how many hours he had spent on Flora Conway's saddle. It had turned out beautiful, trimmed with several bright conches and polished until the leather was a rich oak in color. The leather fender had an ingrained flower design and was trimmed at either edge with a strip of silver. The hobble strap and stirrup were of similar design, as was the cushioned hook for the rider's second leg. When he had finished, the saddle was more comfortable than a good many stuffed chairs.

Allyson recalled the way Flora had walked around the saddle and examined it that very morning. She had looked for faults and found none. When convinced it was probably the finest lady's side-saddle in the entire country, she had told Yancy it would do.

Recalling the moment brought a rise in temperature of Allison's blood. *It would do!* she fumed inwardly. *What a haughty, self-centred snob!*

She had to admit that Flora was the most beautiful woman she had ever seen, but was external beauty so all-important? What about the soul and inner beauty of a person? She was reminded of a wild flower Curly had once shown her. He had said that it was called a bee plant or spider flower. It was beautiful, with pink, bell-shaped flowers and long pods that looked like string-beans. But crush the leaves and it would drive away friends or relatives alike. It was a stinkweed of the most foul variety.

She hated how everyone fawned over a woman for her one obvious asset. What about the fact she had married a man for his money? What did that make her?

Allyson shook the woman from her thoughts. Let men curry favor from Flora as if she was a queen. A few years down the road and she would be a lonely, embittered, self-centred widow. Once she lost her beauty, no one would want her for herself. She had no real personality for it was all show. She was a pretty picture on the wall: no reality, no sense of feeling, no compassion or humanity.

For herself, Allyson tried to think of her future. Once her jail time was up serving Yancy, what then? She had no relatives, no friends, no place in the world to go. She could search for a job, but her training consisted mostly of serving a grouchy old man's every need. How many positions were open for her in that field?

What if no one would hire her? Many people still considered her to be a half-breed. Though she had no Indian blood, there were those who would never believe it. She might end up working in a saloon, waiting on tables and pushing away drunks. She had seen a few of those women over the years. They were mostly hard-faced and bitter inside, women with the dead eyes of long-ago dreams and unfulfilled desires.

Kara mumbled something to her dolly in her sleep. It caused Allyson to smile. How fortunate for the little girl to have Yancy come into her life. After losing her own parents, she recalled a great many nights she had cried, suffering from the loneliness of her life. It seemed a lifetime since her mother had tucked her into bed for the night. She had been a child, eager to grow to an adult. It had all changed with the Indian raid.

A chill ran up her back and caused her to shudder. The memory was still alive, glaringly vivid in her mind's eye. She had been gathering wild currants when the attack came. By the time she reached the house, the Indians had gone. There was blood everywhere and all that remained of her normal life were the mangled bodies of those people she loved the most.

She pulled the covers tightly around her shoulders. It was a dreadful memory that would often flood her senses with a clandestine terror from the past. Many nights, while housed at the saloon storeroom, she had huddled under a single blanket, shivering from the cold and fearful some drunk might push open the door. Battered and teased by the other children her age, Allyson had grown up an outcast and all alone.

Then Curly had come along. He said he had made a wager for her because he needed someone to help with his work. Although more her keeper than a guardian, she respected the fact he had never struck her or let her go hungry.

Allyson wished she could have liked the man, but he kept too much to himself. He never let her get close to him. The one or two times she had spoken to him, he turned her away. He was a loner who neither asked or wanted anything of anyone.

A shadow passed by the crack under the door and

her thoughts turned to the present once more. Yancy turned out the lamp, then opened the door to the bedroom a crack, so some of the heat from the banked stove would filter into the room. She listened to the rustle of his clothing, as he stripped down and climbed into his cot for the night. It was comfortable and warm in his house. Mostly, she was comfortable around him.

She wondered if he might let her stay, once her debt was paid for attacking the marshal. He needed help with the store, and Kara was not old enough to take on the chores of keeping house and doing the cooking.

The more she contemplated the idea, the more she became convinced she had to be invaluable to Yancy. If she could learn some of the leather trade, he might keep her on as an employee. It was a possibility she would exploit. Sleep beckoned, but she resisted. She made a silent vow to work on the prospect of earning a place in Yancy's business. A slender smile played along her lips. *Yes, and maybe also a place in his heart!*

Jay Slone looked over the sales record and did some figures on a piece of paper. Then he slid it towards Yancy. 'Ten per cent of the sales . . . and the tax due on your employee.'

Yancy looked at the total and frowned. 'Miss Jenkins is working for fifty cents a day against a fine that was paid to the city of Pine Junction.'

'That makes her an employee. You are required to pay ten per cent of her wages.'

'I see.'

'And don't forget the tax due on your property is coming up next month. There are taxes for this business and the house you are renting.'

'I'm renting both places. The owner is the one responsible for the taxes on their property, not the tenant.'

'Don't work that way in Pine Junction, Nodean. Whoever resides or operates within a given house or structure is responsible for the taxes.'

'I see,' he replied again, growing more irate with each word. 'And how much do these taxes run?'

'Simple mathematics,' the marshal grinned. 'Ten per cent of the estimated value.'

'Each year?' Yancy was incredulous. 'You expect ten per cent each year?'

'It makes it simple to keep track of the taxes that way,' Slone replied. 'We listed your business at about three-hundred dollars. That means you'll owe thirty dollars for it. The house is only valued at a couple hundred. Add in another twenty for that.'

'Anything else?'

'One other tax that comes at the end of each Fall. It is assessed on your inventory.'

'Say what?' Yancy had never heard of such a thing.

'That's right. You make up an inventory of your goods and we tax on the value of merchandise you have on hand.'

'Let me guess – ten per cent of the worth.'

Slone's lips parted in another of his grins. The light in his eyes showed that he enjoyed pushing or taunting people. He did not reply in words, but gave his head an

affirmative nod and queried: 'You got the money due
for this week?'

Yancy counted out the cash and watched the man
leave the store. He was aware of Kara and Allyson
moving up behind him.

'I wonder if Calvin and the others can move up the
elections? We are going to be broke in a matter of
weeks. I don't think I can bring in enough money to
pay the taxes!'

'These killers will not give up without a fight, Yancy.'

There was an odd stir which quelled his turmoil of
anger. She probably had not intended to call him by his
first name. To that point, she had always been formal.
He glanced over his shoulder at Allyson, saw the flush
of her cheeks and smiled inwardly.

'There are some good people in Pine Junction,
Allyson.' He didn't make mention of her slip. 'Once
united together, we'll make this a nice town in which to
live.'

She recovered from her chagrin but was still dispir-
ited. 'I only know when Curly stood up to Slone, he was
killed. I'm afraid anyone who tries to oppose Slone and
the others will end up the same way.'

Yancy did not say so, but he had no misgivings either.
As soon as Slone and Conway learned of the plan to put
a new man in office, war would be declared.

'Some things are worth fighting for,' he said, after a
long pause. 'If need be, we'll use whatever force it takes
to rid this town of a leech like Hilton Conway.'

There was a sadness to Allison's voice. 'You'll all end
up like Curly.'

'I never knew your friend, Curly,' he said, with a conviction in his voice, 'but in a fight I pride myself on two things – I'm a slow man to rile and a hard man to kill.'

The storm Yancy feared was not long in coming. Judge Mantie posted a notice of the upcoming election. The date set was five weeks in the future. The ballot was open for names of perspective candidates. Before the end of the first day, Cal Smith's name had been scribbled on a number of signs.

It happened to be the first of the month, so that brought in a number of soldiers from Fort Grant. Business was good for Yancy. The troopers were a free-spending bunch and spread their cash all over Pine Junction. In turn, some of the people in town ordered or purchased things for themselves.

To Yancy's surprise and delight, Allyson took a keen interest in his work and was a quick learner. Within a short time, she was doing some of the simpler tasks. Once she started a project, she was tenacious and wouldn't quit until finished.

Kara helped too. She swept the floor in the store each day. Then, one afternoon, a passing sheep herder offered a pup from one of his dogs in trade for a rain slicker; Yancy could not refuse. That ended Kara's enthusiasm for working in the store.

The pup was a white shepherd-mix, with big floppy ears and a tail which never ceased wagging. He was a typical mutt, but he was the object of Kara's attention and love from the moment she saw him.

'What's his name?' she asked, cradling the pup in her arms. 'He's got real pretty brown eyes.'

'He's your dog, Kara,' Yancy said, smiling at the scene. 'Call him whatever you want.'

'How about Bunny? He's 'bout as cute as a wittle bunny.'

Yancy lifted an eyebrow. 'You want to call your dog a rabbit?'

'No,' she was indignant. 'Bunny.'

'That's a sorry name for a dog.'

'You said he was mine,' she reminded him. 'You said I could call him anything I wanted.'

'Bunny is a cute name,' Allyson said from a step away.

'See?' Kara challenged. 'Allie likes it.'

Yancy lifted his hands in a show of defeat. 'OK, fine, I like it too, Kara. Bunny is a fine name for a dog. I'm sure he'll be the toughest dog in town with a name like that.'

'He don't got to be tough. He just has to be a good doggie.' She looked up at Yancy expectantly. 'Can I go play with Bunny?'

'Put on your coat and you can take him out behind the store and let him sniff around. When we get him home, we'll make a place for him to sleep.'

'I already got that picked out.'

'Oh yeah?'

She smiled – the way she smiled each time she wrapped him around her little finger. 'He can sleep at the foot of me and Allie's bed. He'll keep our feet warm and we'll keep him warm.'

Yancy might have argued, but it was a debate he

knew he could not win. He decided it was less of a defeat to accept the proposal right off.

'Good idea. That will save me building him a dog house.'

Kara turned with her prize and hurried out the back of the store. When the little girl had vanished from sight, Yancy noticed Allyson was regarding him with an amused look on her face.

'You're a good father,' she said.

'I've a spoiled child on my hands,' he returned. 'I wonder how I can ever put my foot down against her.'

Her expression sobered at once. 'A child needs to be spoiled sometimes. It makes them feel special. I know.'

He could tell she was serious. It twisted and tugged at his heart strings, finding such an envious expression on her face. He realized that Allyson was little more than a child herself in many ways. Her youth had been stolen from her. She had been forced to be strong at a very young age.

'Your dress is beginning to look like the rags you were wearing the day I hired you.'

He could see Allison's gratitude for his choice of words. There was a marked pride in being *hired*, rather than being indentured. She looked down at the dirty smudges on her dress and fingered a mended tear at one seam.

'I'm sorry. I guess I haven't been as careful as I should have been. I'll. . . .'

'It isn't your fault,' he cut her short. 'You've been working sixteen hours a day. You should have more than one dress. I don't know what my mind has been on lately.'

'This one does me fine. I don't want you spending money on me.'

He looked at his timepiece. 'It's time for lunch. Put the closed sign in the window and let's go over to Tompkins' general store. We'll barter for you a dress. He was looking at some boots the other day. I'll bet we can work something out.'

He was rewarded with a timid smile. 'If you say so, Yancy.'

'I'll tell Kara to take Bunny home and wait for us. You lock the front door and meet me at the store.'

Allyson hurried to do as she was told. Yancy went out the back and found Kara giggling and rolling on the ground with her new playmate. The pup was not much larger than a half-grown rabbit, but he was energetic. He raced around her excitedly, pounced on top of her and licked her face. There was little doubt that Yancy had made a good investment on his trade with the herder.

After sending Kara and the dog homeward, Yancy went through the alley and caught up with Allyson at the front of the general store. His timing was not good.

Zip Lovendaul and Leroy Queen, two of Slone's deputies, were inside the store. They were not buying goods, but pressuring John about the upcoming election.

'You'd better reconsider, Tompkins,' Lovendaul said, meaningfully. 'Hilton owns this town. You get in a shoving match with him and you'll lose everything you got.'

John scowled at them both. 'You boys are supposed to represent the law. As far as I can tell, you're nothing more than tax collectors and glorified servants.'

Lovendaul reached across the counter and grabbed John by his shirt front. He jerked him forward and thrust his jaw up close to the storekeeper's face.

'You'd better listen up, Tompkins. This ain't a request. You keep spouting your support for Smith as our new mayor and you risk the consequences!'

Yancy entered with Allyson on his heels. 'I see you're playing the big boar of the sty, Lovendaul,' he interrupted. 'It fits you – at least the big snout and pig-eyes.' He took a whiff of the air. 'Come to think of it, you smell like you belong in a pig pen too.'

The deputy let go of the storekeeper and glared at Yancy. 'You stay out of this, Nodean. I knocked your block off once, I can do it again.'

Yancy sized up the man. He was a weasel wearing pants and a badge. His dull black eyes suddenly shone with the gleam of anticipation. His fists were doubled at his sides. Like it or not, Yancy had turned the deputy's attention to himself.

'I recall, I had a package in my hands the last time, Lovendaul. Besides which, you took me completely by surprise. I don't think you want to try a second round.'

'Well, let's just see. . . !'

The man swung with his last word, but Yancy ducked back and away. He bumped into Allyson and she quickly hurried out the door.

Lovendaul came after Yancy with a flurry of flying fists, but Yancy had mixed it up a few times. He was cagey enough to let the deputy spend his energy with wild swings, while he retreated outside into the street. There he took his stand.

When the weasel missed with a wild punch, Yancy countered with a shot to the man's face. He stung him with a second poke to the nose, then blasted him flush between the eyes. Before Lovendaul realized he'd been hit, Yancy pounded him twice more and knocked him flat on to his back.

Lovendaul lay dazed, his arms useless at his sides. Yancy drew in a breath of air and stood over the man. The physical exertion caused his blood to pump hard and fast.

'Nodean,' the other deputy said, starting after him, 'you've stepped in it now.'

Yancy turned to the second adversary. 'We're through being pushed, Queen. After the elections, you and the rest of the gunnies on the Conway payroll will be out of work.'

Queen was somewhat larger than Lovendaul. He did not telegraph his punch, but Yancy was ready all the same. The roundhouse grazed his temple, but the bulk of the power missed its mark.

Yancy used his experience as a fighter. He drove at Queen and punished him with his fists. Queen backed away from the attack and crashed into the wall of the mercantile. It caused him to be off balance and his defence was lowered. . . . That was all it took.

Yancy pummeled him with hard blows to the ribs and stomach. Before Queen could recover, he hammered him twice in the face.

Queen squirmed away from the wall and tried to fight back. He was spitting blood and threw out a couple of weak shots. Yancy knew that Lovendaul might be back in the fight at any moment. He dared not wait for his own second wind.

He launched a final brutal assault, knocking Queen back against the wall again. Trapped as he was, the deputy could not ward off a number of Yancy's blows. When he connected with the man's jaw, he saw his eyes glaze. With one hand, he grabbed hold of Queen's shirt and threw him into the street.

Lovendaul had managed to rise to his feet, but he quickly threw his hands out in front of him, palms outward, as if trying to push an invisible force away from him.

'Hold it!' he cried, in a high-pitched voice. 'Hold it, Nodean! We're done!'

Yancy's adrenalin was flowing. He took a menacing step towards Lovendaul and, in the man's hasty attempt to escape, he stumbled and fell over backwards.

'That's it, Nodean!' Jay Slone's voice was as cold as the winter wind. 'You're under arrest!'

Yancy spun around, ready to dismantle the marshal. His knuckles were raw and smeared with blood. He would teach Slone a lesson too. But the marshal had his gun out. He was not fool enough to tackle Yancy with his fists.

'I said you're under arrest,' Slone growled. 'You take another step and I'll spill your guts all over the street!'

Yancy had not worn a gun while in town. It would have made little difference at the moment, for Slone already had his weapon out. To draw against a pointed gun would have been the act of a fool ... one who would have ended up dead real sudden.

'I was defending myself.' He managed a degree of calm in his voice. 'Lovendaul took the first swing.'

'That's right,' John backed up the story. 'Your thugs came in and were threatening me. They tried to do the same to Nodean and he trimmed their branches.'

'The law is the law,' Slone argued. 'No one is allowed to beat up my deputies.'

Chaw Benedict came into view. He had been watching the whole scene from the alley. He spat a stream of tobacco juice into the dirt, before he looked over at Slone.

'Zip and Leroy were the ones who got out of line, Jay. You best rethink bringing charges against the boot-and-saddle man.'

John was quick to side with Chaw. 'You take this before Judge Mantie and your men will lose their jobs, Slone. We've a dozen witnesses to the fact that Lovendaul has been badgering anyone who is supporting Cal for mayor. If someone goes to jail, it'll be your pals!'

Zip Lovendaul had his bandanna up to his bleeding nose. Leroy Queen was still spitting blood from his split lip. Slone wanted reprisal, but he knew when the odds were stacked against his winning. He was forced to back down.

He nonchalantly holstered his gun and grunted. 'All right, Chaw,' he tossed the words off casually, but there was an icy glaze to his eyes. 'Luck is with you, Nodean.

With Chaw backing your story, there won't be any charges this time.' His expression became cold. 'But, I won't put up with brawlers or troublemakers in my town.'

'It won't be your town that much longer,' John told him.

Slone's icy stare went to the storekeeper. 'You talk a good fight, John. We'll see who is still standing when the smoke clears.'

Lovendaul and Queen staggered off to lick their wounds. Slone glared long and hard at both John and Yancy, then followed after them.

'Three coyotes,' John stated simply. 'They won't give up easy.'

'Thanks, Chaw,' Yancy said to the deputy.

He took a moment to roll his tobacco to one cheek and spat a second time. 'No trouble, Nodean. As I recollect, the job of a deputy marshal is to maintain law and order.'

John, Allyson and Yancy remained on the street, while Chaw wandered off toward the jail. As soon as he was out of hearing distance, Yancy spoke to John.

'What do you make of Deputy Benedict?'

The store owner thought for a moment. 'I've mixed feelings about him. He wears a badge for Slone, but I've never known him to cause any trouble. I'd say he is a man who hires his gun but draws the line on what chores he does for the money.'

'Might be worth talking to him privately. We need to know where he stands.'

John showed a wide smile that revealed his crooked

teeth. 'It's no secret where you stand any more, Yancy. You took those two men apart like a busted wheel. I had a hunch you knew how to handle yourself.'

Yancy might have rebuked his words, but Allyson was at his side. She had a kerchief and dabbed at a trickle of blood that came from a small cut at the corner of his mouth. He could not remember being hit there. When lost to the excitement of the fight, he hadn't felt a single punch. Clearly, his own unleashed fury blotted out everything else.

'We came about a dress for the lady here,' he finally told John.

'Come inside, Miss Allyson,' he offered. 'My Emma will help you find something that will fit. As for you, Yancy, I've got some aged Scotch whisky on a shelf behind the counter. A taste of that will take care of your aches and pains.'

'Well, maybe a small taste. I'm not a drinking man.'

John laughed. 'Me neither – at least, not since I married Emma. When I was young and foolish, I used to dip my beak at night and crow like a rooster till sun-up.'

Yancy chuckled and followed him into the store. Emma took Allyson to the rack of clothing and began to sort through different dresses with her.

Yancy wondered if he had made a mistake. He had openly confronted and fought with the law in Pine Junction. The battle lines were drawn. The neutral position of his investigation was lost. He had placed himself squarely on the side of John and the few who dared to oppose Conway's powerful control. He had intended to gather evidence against Hilton for misusing city funds, but he couldn't sit back and wait. He decided he would send off a letter to Konrad and let him know how the situation was progressing. He hoped the marshal didn't decide Yancy had made a mess of things and send him back to prison!

Six

'Hilly,' Flora spoke up, 'did you know that two of our town deputies were beaten to a pulp this morning?'

Hilton Conway sighed. 'Yes, Flora, honey. Zip and Leroy tried to push the saddle-maker around and got their wings clipped.'

Flora came over to stand next to his chair. She was attired in a flowing white satin gown that clung to her womanly charms like wet linen. Her hair was perfectly managed, with not so much as a single strand out of place.

He swallowed a sudden rush of passion, fighting off the urge to jump up and take her into his arms. By the slender smile which played along his wife's lips, she knew exactly how she affected him.

'Isn't there a law against someone beating up lawmen?' she asked.

Hilton forced his mind to function on business matters. 'Queen and Lovendaul overstepped their authority. They were the ones who picked the fight.'

A subtle frown formed on her face. 'I don't like either of them anyway. Queen thinks too much of himself and Lovendaul is always looking at me.'

Her confession sparked a rise in Hilton's blood pressure. 'Looking at you in what way?'

'Oh, nothing indecent, Hilly. It's just that Lovendaul is a crass miscreant and I don't like him. I suppose that's why I object to him looking at me.'

'He better never try anything,' Hilton vowed. 'By Hanna, I'll. . . .'

Flora laughed at his anger and reached out to stroke the side of his face. 'You are a jealous puppy, Hilly. You know I don't spend any time around men like Lovendaul.'

He felt a warm flush from being touched in such a way. Flora only had to smile at him, to place her hand on his, and he was putty for her to mold.

'Do you think John has a chance against you in the elections?' she asked.

'I'm afraid he has a very good chance.'

She showed a serious mien. 'What would that do to you and the coal mine?'

He wished she would speak in *we* terms. He didn't like the separateness in the way she put things. He let it pass and shrugged his shoulders.

'I think I'm close to getting a spur run from the railroad. It usually takes about fifty per cent of up-front money. I have put together a fair sum, but not nearly enough to meet the required needs yet.'

'Perhaps we should take our money and go to some other town. I've always wanted to live in a big city. We

could go to St Louis or San Francisco. You could buy a
big house on a hill and we could go to fine restaurants
and theatres.'

'I would need to earn more money, once we were
there. I've put too much in the mine to back away now.
All we need is for that rail to be run and we will never
have to worry about money again.'

That sparked a renewed brightness into her expression. 'Then you've got to win the election. Make
promises the people want to hear. Tell them how this
rail spur will make them all rich. You can do it.'

The enthusiasm in her voice left no doubt: Flora's
dream was to have more money than she could ever
spend. Material wealth was all important to her. So long
as Hilton could supply her needs, she would remain at
his side.

He put his hand on hers and enjoyed the warmth in
her eyes. He didn't believe she really loved him, but he
could accept that. He was the only man to hold her
close, the only man to kiss those beautiful lips. Surely,
he was the most envied man in all the world.

'I'll take care of it, Flora, honey.'

'I'm sure you will, Hilly.'

She smiled at him and left the room. He could not
keep his eyes from straying after her, enticed by the
natural sway of her walk. He drank in her beauty like an
intoxicating wine. Without reservation, he knew he
would do anything to keep her.

However, he had to win the election first, then bring
the railroad to Pine Junction. He would do it, even if it
meant crawling on his hands and knees through the

fires of Hades. No price was too high to keep Flora for his own!

Chaw Benedict sat with his back to the wall. He sipped a beer and looked up from his cards. Spread out as they were, Yancy deduced that he had been playing solitaire.

Yancy pulled out the chair opposite the deputy. He did not ask for an invite, but sat down and tipped back his hat. 'I don't think you're clay from the same mold as Slone and his two boys. If push comes to shove, I'd like to know where you stand.'

Chaw paused, looking over his cards. He placed a black seven on a red eight and then shook his head. 'I'm a lawman, Nodean. I'm not supposed to take sides.'

'Jay Slone might differ with that opinion.'

'Well, he's the marshal. I'm only a deputy. I'm supposed to follow his orders.'

'What if the order is against the law?'

Chaw gave Yancy a long, hard look. 'You seem to have brought a pile of trouble with you, Nodean. Ever since you arrived, there has been unrest and rebellion. If you are looking to count me into your fold, forget it.'

'I don't want you taking sides, Deputy. The law should protect the citizens of this town. I'm curious if you'll do that, or are you a hired hand for Hilton Conway?'

It was obvious Chaw did not like being put into a corner. He played another card and refused to meet Yancy's challenge. 'It might be a good idea for you to start packing your gun, Nodean. If trouble comes again, you won't get out of it with your fists.'

'Is that a warning?'

He lifted one careless shoulder. 'Call it advice.'

Yancy rose from the table. Chaw ignored him, concentrating on his game. He would not commit himself to support Jay Slone's actions, nor would he take a stand against Yancy and the other people in town. 'The middle of the fence can be real uncomfortable, Chaw. Time's a-coming when you won't be able to remain astride. If you step down, I hope it's on the side of justice.'

'You'd best keep your eyes open too,' Chaw warned him. 'Was I you, I wouldn't sleep with any doors or windows unlocked.'

Yancy turned and walked out of the High Card Saloon. He had not gotten Chaw to take a stand, but even that was a victory. If he didn't blindly support Slone or Hilton, it cut the odds by one. If he joined the side of justice, that would cut the odds by two. Either way, Yancy had done as John had asked.

The night air was cold. He hurried his step, going down the alley towards his house. His thoughts were on the other businessmen. Each had a list of people to visit and ask for support. It was risky, for Hilton could not afford to lose the election. He was bound to be working on a plan of his own to win the race.

Suddenly, Yancy slid to a halt. There was a flashing in the night, a brilliant glow. The bright sky was the culmination of his fears. Calvin Smith's tavern was on fire!

Everett Wade, John Tompkins and several others stood alongside the owner of the burned shell of a building.

Yancy was among them. The air was filled with the acrid smell of ashes and freshly-charred timber. There was nothing left of the tavern.

'Fuel oil is the only thing to cause the wood to burn so hot and fast,' Wade said.

'It was no accident, it was arson!' John declared.

Calvin stared at the remains of his business. He had been wiped out in a matter of minutes. His life's work had gone up in smoke and flames. He groaned. 'I'm broke.'

'You can rebuild and start again,' John told him. 'We'll all pitch in and help.'

'That big stove in the kitchen cost me a bundle. I had trays, dishes, glasses, inventory. The tables and chairs were all especially made for my place. Every dime I had earned was in a box in the attic.' He sounded next to tears. 'I'm flat busted. Ain't no way I'll ever get going again.'

John took hold of his arm. 'You're wrong, Cal. We'll all pitch in and help.'

But Calvin was not going to be consoled. He jerked away and strode wordlessly off into the dark of night.

'I hope he doesn't do something stupid,' Wade said. 'A man who has lost everything might not be thinking straight.'

'I'll stick with him,' John offered. 'You men go on home. I'll see if I can buy Cal a drink or two. Maybe he'll feel a spark of hope by morning.'

The other men left, but Wade and Yancy remained for a time. When the ashes cooled, they searched through the rubble for any clues to the start of the fire.

It was a wasted effort. There was no evidence the fire had been set.

'It's colder than a politician's heart out here, Nodean. If someone used fuel oil, there ain't anything here to prove it.'

'You're right about that. It will only look like a co-incidence that Cal was out trying to gather votes.'

'Wonder if either of our places will be next?'

The two of them stood silently, hands in pockets, arms tucked against their sides for warmth. There was nothing more that could be done for the night.

'Guess I'll head back to the house. Keep an eye open, Wade. You own your business establishment. I don't think anything will happen to either of my places, because I'm renting them both. Hilton might not condone burning down his own properties.'

'That's a point well taken. See you tomorrow, Nodean.'

Yancy pivoted toward his house and went through the darkness. He found Allyson had the lamps burning and the meal was heating on the stove.

'We waited for you,' she said. 'Kara won't eat unless you are home for supper.'

He smiled. 'You mean you can't get her to stop play-ing with that pup long enough to get her to the table.'

Allyson laughed shortly. 'I remember having a kitten once. I couldn't stand to have it out of my sight. I used to sneak it into bed and play with it under the covers.'

'Kara doesn't have to sneak her puppy into bed. I was smart enough not to try and keep her and Bunny apart.'

'Wise choice,' she simpered. 'Give into the child before they ask. That way, you don't lose an argument.'

He grew serious. 'Calvin Smith's place burned to the ground. He lost everything.'

She showed a pained expression. 'How terrible.'

'Can't be certain if it was an accident or if the fire was set. By the time we got a water brigade going, it was too late. Nothing left but ashes.'

'Do you think it was the work of Slone?'

He sighed. 'We have no proof it was set, but it is a distinct possibility.'

'It has started then,' she said. 'There will be a war in Pine Junction, a battle between Hilton supporters and those who back Cal for mayor.'

Yancy shrugged out of his coat. 'Supper smells good.' He changed the subject.

'It's only some stew I tossed into the pot. I'll be glad when the weather warms up and we can start a garden. Stew looks kind of sickly without any vegetables.'

He enjoyed the way she said *we can start a garden*. He quickly hid the feeling. 'Meat and potatoes are fine by me.'

'A child needs vegetables to grow.'

'I suppose you know more about a growing child than I do.'

A sadness flooded Allison's face. 'I was only twelve when my parents died.'

Yancy felt a surge of compassion rush through him. Allyson had lived through a nightmare existence. He wondered how she ever managed to smile. For a moment, his eyes met her own. There was an odd sort of hunger embedded in the depths of her gaze. It was not for want of food, more of a yearning. He wondered what she was thinking.

'Hey!' Kara had come over and was looking up at them both. 'Are you two going to stand there staring at each other, or are we going to eat? I'm starved, and Bunny is so hungry that he has been trying to eat my shoes.'

They gathered at the table and Kara said grace. Before Yancy had taken a half-dozen bites, there came a knocking at the door. He opened it to find Everett Wade standing there. The look on his face told Yancy there had been more trouble.

'What's happened?'

'Cal is dead. He went calling on Hilton and Slone gunned him down.'

Yancy felt his stomach roll. He was instantly assailed by a wave of emptiness. 'I thought John was going to stick with him?'

'Cal pretended to go home. John went to tell his wife that he was going to spend a few hours with Cal. By the time he got back, Cal had taken his gun and gone up to Hilton's house.'

'And Slone just happened to be waiting for any trouble that might arise?'

'Yeah, he probably figured there would be some backlash over the fire. Cal didn't even get his gun clear of its holster. Slone plugged him three times.' Disgust was thick in his voice. 'Three times! He was taking no chances.'

'How did John take it?'

'He blames himself, but I should have been the one

to go with Cal. I don't have a wife or kids to split my time with.'

'I didn't think Cal was fool enough to do exactly what Hilton and Slone wanted. By getting himself killed, we've lost our candidate for mayor.'

'It was a fool stunt and it shows how far Hilton will go to win re-election.'

'What can I do?'

'Nothing at the moment. I thought you ought to know what happened.'

'Thanks for coming by, Wade. If you'd care for a bite to eat, we have plenty.'

'I appreciate the offer, but I've got to get back and keep an eye on my place.' He patted the gun on his hip. 'I'm not the shot I was before I broke my hand, but they won't catch me sleeping. If Slone or his boys come looking for trouble, I'll salt their backsides.'

'We've got to stick together on this. Cal acted on his own and it got him killed. If there is any other action to be taken, we need to be organized.'

'I hear you, Nodean. I won't do anything stupid.'

'See you tomorrow.'

Wade went back out into the night. Yancy closed the door and slid home the bolt. Instead of returning to the table, he added some wood to the stove. Light steps approached and Allyson was at his side.

'Calvin is dead?' she asked softly.

'Slone shot him. It sounds as if Cal went to Hilton's house with a gun. He obviously blamed him for the fire.'

'Do you think Hilton gave the order to burn down his place?'

'I don't know the man, but he stands to lose a lot of money if he loses control of this town. He might even lose his chance to bring in the railroad.'

'He would lose something more important,' Allyson said. 'He would lose Flora.'

Yancy glanced at her. 'You think she is his main concern?'

'When I was in jail, I heard Slone talk about her to the other deputies. She is the only thing in the world that Hilton wants total ownership to. Every dime he earns is spent to make her happy. Nothing she asks for is denied her. I think Hilton will do anything to keep her in luxury and riches. It's the only way he can maintain his hold on her.'

Yancy recalled watching the two of them. Hilton fawned over Flora much the same as Bunny did around Kara. His wanting to keep her at his side was not the adoring love of a devoted husband, but the conspicuous pride of ownership.

'I wonder if I did you a favor by employing you, Allyson. If this escalates into a war, you and Kara might be in real danger.'

It was a subtle act, but one Yancy noticed at once. The young woman rested her hand on his arm. 'Don't concern yourself about me. I'm not worth worrying about.'

He was instantly angered by her remark. 'Don't you ever say that, Allyson,' his voice was sharp. 'Don't sell yourself short. You're a very special person.'

She ducked her head. 'You know what I mean.' Her voice was subdued until Yancy could barely pick up the words. 'After the life I've lived. . . .'

Yancy had not spent much time around women. He did not know how to sweet talk them. It was an awkward gesture, taking hold of her arms and pulling her forward, as if to shake some sense into her. He was ill-prepared for the result of such an action.

He jerked a little too hard and threw her off balance. Allyson was unable to catch herself and came against him with such force that he was knocked backward. He stumbled over his own feet and sat down on the floor, pulling her down on top of him.

Allyson halfway caught herself with her hands but still ended up sitting on Yancy's lap. Surprised, she giggled and regarded him with a glowing smile.

'Guess I showed you,' Yancy quipped, a little self-consciously.

Allyson giggled again. 'You certainly know how to sweep a girl off of her feet.'

'What'cha doing?' Kara asked, hurrying over from the table. 'Can I play too?'

Without awaiting an answer, she climbed up on to Allison's back. Then the three of them were rolling on the floor, wrestling and laughing. Forgotten were the deadly events of the evening and the dangers which might lay ahead. It was a release of pent-up emotions, a chance for each of them to think only of the joy of being together.

The sun shone brightly upon the newly turned earth. The snow had all melted, except for a few shady spots. The ground remained frozen in places, but the grave had been dug without too much extra effort.

Calvin Smith was laid to rest in a crude pine box. The marker was a wooden slab, with neatly-etched letters. John Tompkins' wife had worked several hours to carve his name and the date of his passing. The words were to the point. *Calvin Smith, born 1835. A good, honest man – killed by Jay Slone, 1875.*

The faction supporting Hilton Conway was conspicuously absent. The only lawman to put in an appearance was Chaw Benedict. Even he stood back as an observer, not mixing with the mourners. He wore his badge and gun, so it was difficult to tell if he came out of respect, curiosity, or if he had been ordered to keep an eye on the funeral.

'Calvin Smith died for each and every one of us,' John spoke solemnly. 'He supported the idea of sensible taxes, a nice town, with everyone contributing to the welfare of the other person. His courage to run for office of mayor is what got him killed.

'We know now we can't hope to win a gun-fight against the powerful tyrant and gunmen who run this town. The only action we can take in the name of our dear friend, Calvin Smith, is at the election. Remember this brave man when you vote next week . . . for me.' John heaved a deep breath. 'I'm running for mayor in Cal's place.'

Yancy swept the faces of the crowd. There was an odd mixture of expressions among them. Some were sad and forlorn, while others glowed with a renewed determination. These were hearty pilgrims, used to the never-ending battle against the Indians, bandits and the worst weather Nature had to offer. The future was in their hands and they were willing to accept the challenge. Hilton Conway's days as the power of the valley were numbered.

As the meeting broke up, Chaw intercepted Yancy. He touched the tip of his hat in a gentlemanly manner to Allyson. 'Could I have a moment alone with you, Nodean?'

'I'll go on to the store,' she offered. 'You still want to open this afternoon?'

'Yes,' he answered. 'I'll be along in a few minutes.'

Chaw watched her hurry along the walk. When he turned back to Yancy, he had the thread of a smile on his lips. 'Who would have ever thought there was such a pretty young woman under all of those dirty rags?'

'No one ever gave her the chance to be a woman. I have to admit I wasn't real impressed the first time I saw her in your jail.'

Chaw chuckled. 'No, I think not. Scrubbing the floor like an old washer-woman, dressed in those smelly rags, she didn't look like anything special.'

'Something on your mind?'

The man grew instantly serious. 'Trouble is brewing, Nodean. I feel it coming.'

'You're right, deputy. Calvin was the first to die, but he won't be the last.'

'You are on the list,' Chaw told him, carefully. 'You and John are the catalysts behind the election. Hilton can't lose this race. He needs to keep taxing people for the railroad line. If he is beaten for mayor, he'll be ruined. There can be no doubt that Slone will try and influence you and force John to drop from the race.'

'Why are you telling me this?'

The man let out a lengthy sigh. 'Guess I'm not very smart.'

'Slone and Hilton see you warning me, they might think you have stepped down from that fence you were riding . . . on the wrong side.'

Chaw pulled a plug of chewing tobacco from his back pocket. Before speaking, he took a deliberate bite from the Liggett & Myers Tobacco plug. 'I started chewing this stuff back when it was made by J.E. Liggett & Brother. Never did know the first names of those fellows. They haven't changed anything in their product that I can tell.'

'Nasty habit,' Yancy said. 'I'm glad I never took up chewing.'

Chaw shifted the bite into his cheek and grinned. 'Makes you tough, Nodean. Swallow enough tobacco juice and you get meaner than a scalded grizzly bear.'

'I can believe that.'

Chaw looked at the fresh grave and his expression darkened. 'Think of Cal before you go up against Slone. He isn't all that fast on the draw, but he is deceptive. I heard the boys talking about the killing last night. Calvin was primed for a fight, but he was taken by surprise when Slone gunned him down. Like I said, he's deceptive.'

'I'll remember.'

Chaw walked away without another word. Yancy did not know how far the man would go to back up his badge. Slone was still the marshal. However, it might give him an ally, should he produce his own badge and start arresting people.

Returning home first, before going to the store, Yancy wondered how to proceed. He didn't know beans about doing detective work. Perhaps he should have figured a way to stop Hilton, before he was able to burn out Cal and have him killed.

Yet, how did he prove misuse of the city's funds? Was it enough to have the taxes beyond reason? Would that stand up before a court of law?

Kara ran from the house with Bunny right behind. She waved and called out to him. The puppy yapped and bounced behind her, his ears flopping, tail wagging.

'Hi, my girl,' he said, reaching down to catch her in his arms. He lifted her up and swung her around. 'What's my angel been up to?'

She laughed and beamed at him with her bright eyes. 'Me and Bunny been chasing a chipmunk. You ought to see him. Bunny's a real hunter!'

'I can imagine,' he replied.

'Bet he's the best dog in the whole town.'

'Can't be any doubt about that. He's got you to train him.'

'Is it OK for us to play outside a little longer?'

Yancy set her down and smiled at the way the pup was right at her feet. He again patted himself on the back for making such a good investment by trading for the pup.

'I suppose so. I've got some work to do, but Allyson will be coming home to prepare supper in a little while.'

'She's nice, ain't she.' It was a statement. 'I'll bet she'd be a good mother.'

'What makes you say that?'

Kara had a look of total innocence on her face. 'Oh, you know, Daddy. It's one of them things . . . a *hunches*!' she declared. 'I got a *hunches* about her.'

'Oh, you do, huh?'

'Yep.' Then she became totally candid. 'Are you gonna ask her to marry you?'

Yancy's teeth about fell out. 'Well.' He had to clear his throat, searching for words. 'Allyson has a life of her own to live. A woman needs time to think, time to plan what she wants. Allyson has been tending and serving to someone's needs most of her life. I think she deserves a chance to figure out what she really wants.'

Kara was her usual blunt self. 'I gots another *hunches* that she wants you!'

Yancy tried to hide his chagrin at the statement. He reached out and took her hands in his own. 'You have to be careful what you say around Allyson. If you said something like that, she might be embarrassed.'

'What's 'barrassed mean?'

'You know, like falling down on a slippery floor and having people laugh at you.'

'Oh, yeah. You mean when your face gets red and you hate it.'

'That's right.'

'Allie has never done nothing to 'barrass me. I asked her if she wanted to be my mommy and she smiled at me and said it would be very nice.'

He let out a sigh of exasperation. 'Why don't you take Bunny back to the house? I need to get over to the store.'

'Sure, I can do that. Bunny follows me everywhere. He knows he's my dog.'

'I'll see you at supper then.'

Kara called for Bunny and ran back towards their house. Yancy stood and watched her, filled with a warm satisfaction. It was hard to recall how empty his life had been before she entered it.

'Nice kid.' Jay Slone's voice destroyed the serenity of the moment. 'Be a shame if she lost a second father.'

Yancy rotated enough to put a hard look on the marshal. Slone was confident to the point of being cocky. It was an attitude that begged to have someone remove the feather stuffing from his pillow.

'We said farewell to a good man a few minutes ago, Slone. Calvin was an honest citizen and God-fearing man. You had no right to gun him down.'

Slone appeared offended. 'I was only doing my job, Nodean. He was crazy over losing his place and wanted to kill Hilton Conway. I tried to reason with him, but he wouldn't listen.'

'So you killed him.'

There was an unholy fire burning in the depths of his gaze. 'I have what you might call a vested interest in the railroad, Nodean. If tracks are laid up here, I stand to make a lot of money. Lovendaul and the others work for wages, but I've got a bigger stake in all of this. Conway agreed to a percentage deal with me. You might say it's imperative to both of us that we see the railroad come into Pine Junction.'

'There are other ways to raise money, Slone. If you've got a sound investment, get a bank or the railroad to back you. No one has to twist the arms of investors to get the tracks laid to the gold-producing towns or major cities.'

'Coal is not so much in demand,' Slone replied. 'There's still a lot of competition throughout the country. Once the demand grows, we'll be rich from that black gold.'

'And if you get the railroad and still can't compete, you'll end up broke.'

Slone grinned, the light bright in his eyes. 'I intend for us to have that chance, Nodean. You've got yourself a nice family. Don't risk losing them over this issue.'

Yancy stood erect and held Slone with an icy glare. 'I don't take kindly to threats, Slone. You start prodding me, I'll come back at you like a stung mule.'

Slone let his eyes roam over him, as if sizing him up anew. The burning within his gaze remained steady, but his facial muscles relaxed. 'You don't push easy . . . I like that. Too many people grow fat and lazy once they get a family or their own business. They are afraid of losing what they have and will do anything to keep it.'

'I shucked my hobbles at a young age, Slone. I've been my own man for a long time. If it comes to a fight, I won't be the easy prey Smith was.'

'You ought to consider backing Conway, Nodean. We could cut you a break on your taxes and maybe let you in on a percentage of the coal mine.'

'You can't push me and I don't bribe, Slone. Anything else you want?'

The man laughed. 'It'll be a shame to have to kill you, Nodean. I like your style.'

'I can't return the compliment, Slone,' he retorted.

His words did not seem to matter to the marshal. He spun about and walked away, still chuckling to himself. Even that reaction was enough to make a man nervous. Was he so self-confident that he didn't worry about another man's skill with a gun? Or was he more a man who enjoyed a challenge and saw Yancy as a worthy adversary?

Either way, it was worrisome. He had pitted himself against Slone. It was only a matter of time before the two of them met on a field of battle. Considering the experience of a man like Slone, that was not a pleasant thought.

Seven

Hilton paced the room and stopped to confront Slone. They were alone in the marshal's office. 'Then you don't think we have the votes to carry the election?'

'I can't buy or scare some of the men. A good many of them fought in the war between the Union and Confederacy. If they get their hackles up, we might end up with a fight we can't win.'

'What about the women? Wyoming has always counted women's votes. Do you think there's any way we can use their numbers to our advantage?'

'Most women will vote with their husbands. That doubles the odds against us.'

'Then we've got to change the odds.'

Slone frowned, obviously not understanding his train of thought. 'How do we manage that?'

'We should warn the women that violence and bloodshed might erupt if I lose the election. Many of them will want to protect their men from harm.'

'I don't think we can count on Chaw for something like that. He works for the high wages you pay, but he balks at crossing over the line and breaking any laws. We might have to send him packing.'

'His gun adds to our weight. How about we offer him more money?'

'The man has his own code of ethics,' Slone replied. 'I don't know how far he'll go if this gets nasty.'

'How about the others?'

'Zip and Leroy can speak privately to some of the wives and other eligible women. They will do whatever we tell them to do. Anything else?'

'Bring in a half-dozen women and some new dealers and such to work at the King's Full Saloon. Hire some extra workers at the mine; or around town. Get as many new people as you can and work them until the election. We need the votes.'

Slone blinked in surprise. 'You think that'll work?'

'The tavern burned down. That means there are customers out there to be taken care of – especially the soldiers from the fort. We'll hurt Wade's saloon with new girls too. Get the best you can find in Cheyenne or wherever and promise them top dollar.'

'Where do we get the money for all of this?'

'We'll use the funds we have saved up for the railroad. The saloon will pay back a sizeable portion of dividends on our investment.'

'I thought Flora was against dance-hall gals?'

'She knows the price of failure in my bid for this election. If we lose the office of mayor, you and I will be broke.'

'John and the others won't stand still over this. They'll know what we're doing.'

'There's nothing anyone can do about it.'

'Is there a law about how long a body has to be a resident before they can vote?'

'As mayor, I can state that anyone who earns a living in Pine Junction is allowed the privilege of voting. All we have to do is have enough miners, workers, bartenders and girls to win the election.'

'I've done some figuring and know about how many votes we need.'

'Good, if we can intimidate a few women and hire the extra people, we should have enough people to sway the votes in our favor.'

'We don't have long. Judge Mantie set the date as the first of next month.'

'That gives us plenty of time. I want those girls and workers here by next week.'

Slone whistled. 'That is pushing things awfully fast.'

'Can you do it?'

'I've a cousin in Cheyenne. He can probably round up the hired help for us and have them here in a few days. Me and the boys can also spend some time talking to the local citizens. We can probably get a few to see things our way.'

'We only need a few, Slone.'

'It's going to take a lot of money to pull this off, Hilton. We are risking everything on this election.'

'We don't have a choice. If I'm beaten, you'll be out of a job too. We will be sitting here with a thousand tons of coal and no way to transport it to market.'

'I'm with you, Hilton. I've got my stake in this too. Be sure you don't forget about my percentage.'

'Help get me elected for another term and we'll both end up rich.'

Slone smiled. It was a rare smile, not the wicked grin that usually curled his lips. 'I like the sound of that, Hilton. I've never been a greedy man. All I want is more money than I'll ever need.'

'We're both going to put everything on the line, Slone. It's all or nothing.'

'I'll head for Cheyenne tomorrow, just as soon as I get the boys outlined on their jobs.' He paused. 'I'll be needing some money.'

Hilton nodded. 'You come by the house. I'll give you a thousand dollars. That ought to hire all the people we need.'

'I'll bring back an army,' he said.

Hilton went out of the office and was joined at once by Flora. She had been shopping at the general store. There was a tightness about her mouth and worry lines above her brow.

'What did he say?' she asked at once.

'He'll ride to Cheyenne tomorrow. I roughly estimate that we need a hundred votes to win the election. With our supporters, the miners and my employees, I believe we have about eighty solid votes already.'

'The rest of the people in Pine Junction are fools,' she said, angrily. 'Don't they understand the railroad would bring in money and prosperity for all of them?'

'Some refuse to look to the future, my dear. I hope this little scheme is enough to win the election. Everything we have is riding on this one big play.'

Flora put on her winning smile. 'I love a big spender,

Hilly. Men who will risk everything they have on a spin of the wheel are so exciting to be around.'

Hilton enjoyed the woman's beauty. The way she smiled at him made his blood heat up. He knew she was telling the truth. She liked a man who took chances to win. The problem was, he didn't think she was the kind of woman to stick by a man if he lost. So long as he was a winner, she would remain at his side. That made the gamble to stay in office even greater. If he lost the election, he stood to lose much more than the railroad spur. He might lose Flora.

'We'll win on this roulette wheel, my dear,' he said, with a confidence he did not really feel. 'If all goes as planned, you'll get your shopping trip to Denver this summer. By next year, the railroad will be shipping our coal. We'll go back east to the new opera theatre in New York. We'll mingle with royalty.'

The glow in Flora's eyes warmed his heart. He could see how the words affected her. She was lost to the promise of riches and glamour.

'You are such a wonderful husband, Hilly. I'm proud to be your wife.'

He beamed at the praise, his head held high and proud. She was worth every bit of his effort. He would do whatever was needed to make her happy. If that meant buying an election, he would do it – anything to keep her happy.

The opposing factions in town began to split Pine Junction in two. Most residents were sick of endless promises and out-of-sight taxes. They had no desire to become a shipping point for coal. Some thought the end of the tracks usually meant a town full of undesirables.

On the other side were those businesses which would profit from a rail spur. The farmers could ship produce, the cattlemen could ship cattle. It seemed favorable to their side to have the railroad and they were willing to contribute taxes to that end.

There were a number of fights in town. It was not confined to a few hot-headed men. Two women got into a battle at John's store and about wrecked it. Kids were also mixed into the volatile atmosphere. They fought and threw rocks through windows. The war was mounting with each incident.

Parlor girls arrived at the King's Full and there was an immediate increase in fights and revelry. As soon as word spread to the fort, the casino-bar was doing several times the business of Everett Wade's High Card Saloon. Worse than the singing and dancing girls, there was a new idea in play – credit to residents!

Wade was discussing the subject with Yancy at his shop. 'I can't compete with them,' he complained. 'If they owe money to the saloon, they keep going back to try and get even. I'll wager Hilton is going to forgive debts if he wins the election!'

'The mayor must be spending a fortune to do this. It's the act of a desperate man.'

'He's desperate all right, but the moves he's making are those of a crafty old fox. He hired sixteen new employees. All of them will be able to vote in the next election.'

'Who is the new guy managing the place?'

'Hilton brought in Clayton Slone, the marshal's cousin,' he answered, sourly. 'He's no gun hand, but he and his hired help will side with Jay and his boss.'

'How does this affect the election? Does it give Hilton the votes to win?'

Wade rubbed his chin thoughtfully. 'I don't really know, Yancy. We held a sizeable edge before, but this is going to make it close. Even the people who resent the taxes think the railroad is a good idea. Our stand against the taxes looks more like a negative stand against the railroad.'

'We need some way to turn the voters back to the issues at hand. We have to make them remember Cal Smith. They must not forget the way the law in this town makes their own rules. What about the sky-high prices they pay because of the ridiculous taxes? Have they got such short memories that they forget all those things?'

'I don't know, Nodean. I agree with you completely.' He let out an exasperated sigh. 'But how do we get the people – the voters – to think before they vote?'

Yancy thought for a long moment. 'I've an idea that might help.'

'I'm listening.'

'Make a list of all the bad things which have happened in the last couple years under our fine mayor and his hired guns. Make sure you put down the killing of Cal Smith and Allyson's guardian. List the different kinds and high rate of taxes as compared to any other town. Write down anything you can think of that will remind the voters of the kind of lopsided justice we have in this town.'

'Then what?'

'I'm going to make a trip to Cheyenne. I'll get some posters and handbills printed up while I'm there. We'll spread them all over town and give them to every farmer and rancher within voting distance. We have to show the railroad isn't worth the price tag.'

'What about your store?'

'Allyson can run it while I'm gone. She can take the orders and sell what I have on hand. It'll only take me three or four days.'

'Risky business, Nodean. Don't tell anyone what you have in mind. If Slone got word of such a move, he might decide to take you out of the picture. Bringing in girls to his saloon shows Hilton will go to any lengths to win this battle. Flora has always been opposed to dance-hall girls. For him to hire them is an admission of his desperation.'

'We can't let him win, Wade. Somehow, we have to win the election and give this town back to its people.'

'I agree with you, Nodean, but it'll be dangerous every step of the way.'

'The fireworks might explode when I return and we start handing out posters. Be sure you list everything you can think of. We need to remind the people of Pine Junction that we aren't simply opposing the railroad.'

'I'll get with John and write up the list. We should have it ready in an hour.'

'Good. That will give me time to speak to Allyson and get my team in harness.'

'You can take my blood bay mare, Nodean. She's as fast in a sprint as any horse in the country and long on bottom. No need taking a rig that will slow you down and confine you to using the main trails.

'All right, Wade. I appreciate it.'

The man hurried off to complete his task. Yancy looked at his timepiece and gauged how long he had to get things in order. Even as he turned for his store, he was aware of Zip Lovendaul standing across the street watching.

'Keep your eyes open, Deputy,' he said, under his breath. 'I'm going to do a vanishing act that will have you wondering what happened right sudden.'

'We've got a fox sniffing around the hen house, Slone. I don't know what's up, but Wade and Nodean were doing some serious palavering. Next thing I know, Wade is hustling off to John's place and Nodean is picking up supplies from the general store.'

Jay Slone leaned back on the chair behind his marshal's desk. He ran a finger along the scar near his temple thoughtfully, before replying to Lovendaul's report.

'You think they hatched themselves some kind of scheme?'

'Can't be no doubt about it. There was purpose to the way Nodean went to the store. I slipped over and seen Wade's swamper go over to the stable. He saddled that big red mare of his.'

Slone stood up and crossed to the window of the office. 'You think the two of them are going someplace?'

'I couldn't follow both of them. Once Nodean headed for his house, I went to see what Wade was up to. It's for sure the two of them have something up their sleeve.'

'I don't like it. That Nodean is a crafty sort. I don't trust him one bit.'

'What about Wade?'

'Wade is predictable. He's more like a bull than a coyote. He'll come at you from the front. You know where he stands. But Nodean . . . I ain't figured him out yet. He's a man who will use his wits to beat you.'

'He ain't no slouch with his fists either,' Lovendaul said, rubbing his jaw in remembrance of his beating.

'Slip out quietly and saddle your bronc. I want you to tail Wade or Nodean – whichever one leaves town. If they both ride out, you stick with our saddle-maker. He's the brains behind their scheme.'

'Then what?'

'Try and find out what they're up to. If possible, report back to me before you do anything on your own.'

'Right.'

'Take some grub with you. No telling what those two have planned.'

Lovendaul rushed out to do as he was told. Slone remained at the window and watched the street. He hated to send Lovendaul out on a job alone. The man was about as sharp as an inflated balloon. If it came to thinking on his own, they could all be in trouble.

On the other hand, he had to know what Wade and Nodean had in mind. The opposition had to offset the new voters or swallow defeat in the upcoming election.

Even as he considered what steps Nodean might be going to take, he recounted their own plans. Queen had spoken to a number of wives and warned them how it might be dangerous for Hilton to lose the election. They had plied the men with free liquor at the saloon, and Flora had given a party for the ladies and gentlemen who were loyal to their side. They had done about everything they could to ensure victory.

But would it be enough? he wondered. What did Nodean have in store for them? What was his next move?

'Just me and Allie, Daddy?' Kara asked. 'Where you going?'

'It's only for a few days. I'll be back before you know it.'

She gave her small head a negative shake. 'I already know it.'

He took her into his arms and squeezed her tight. 'It'll just be for four days, Kara. This is something I have to do.'

'Can't I go too?'

'I wish I could take you, but you have to take care of Bunny. He's too small to take along.'

She sighed. 'Being 'sponsible is hard sometimes. I guess you're right, Daddy.'

'I knew you'd understand.'

'Did you tell Allie?'

'I'm about to do that now.' He kissed her on the cheek. 'Be a good girl and help her while I'm gone.'

'Sure, Daddy,' she showed her toothless smile. 'I'll take care of her and Bunny.'

'How about taking Bunny out for his morning exercise? I'll speak to Allyson and explain what is going on.'

'Come on, Bunny!' she called. The pup was right on her heels, as she went out of the house. Even as the door closed, Allyson came from the kitchen.

'There's some tins of beans, hard rolls and jerky in your saddle-bags.' She held it out for him to take. 'It isn't much.'

He hooked the saddle-bag over his shoulder and smiled. 'It'll be fine.'

'You're going to do something dangerous. I can feel it.'

'Not really. I have to go to Cheyenne. I'll be back in four days or less.'

'It has to do with the upcoming election don't it?' She lowered her eyes, when he didn't answer. 'I keep thinking of Curly when he tried to fight Slone. I . . . I don't want anything to happen to you.'

Yancy reached out and put a hand on her arm. 'Nothing is going to happen to me, Allyson. This is a job I have to do. I promised a man to strip Hilton from power. Once we have a new mayor and the taxes are mostly gone, I'll be able to think of the future.'

'I don't understand,' Allyson said.

'I didn't come to Pine Junction by accident,' he admitted. 'I came to put an end to the tyranny here.'

Allyson lifted her head. Yancy was moved to see there were tears in her eyes. She shook her head slightly. 'You can't fight Slone. He'll kill you, the way he killed Cal Smith and Curly. I – I'm afraid for you.'

He let the saddle-bags drop to the floor and took her
into his arms. He intended to console her, but something went haywire. The next thing he knew, his lips
were on her own. Not only did he kiss her, but she
kissed him right back.

He felt the uncertainty, the fear, the childlike innocence in that single embrace. It lasted only a fleeting
moment, before Allyson recovered and withdrew. He
reluctantly let her step back, but he yearned to keep
her in his arms.

'I . . . that is . . . I mean. . . .' But Allyson could not
seem to locate the right words. Yancy picked up his
goods and recovered his composure. The fire in his
blood threatened to stop the flow of his own words. He
swallowed the rise of passion and cleared his throat.

'I'm sorry, Allyson. I didn't mean to do that.'

She flicked a sharp glance at him, a slight frown
furrowed her brow. 'You didn't mean it?'

'No!' he retracted the statement quickly. 'That isn't
what I wanted to say.'

'You don't have to say anything.' Her voice was cool
and level.

He let out a groan. 'No! Allyson! The fact is, I've
wanted to do that for a long time . . . kiss you, I mean.
But I didn't want to . . . to take advantage of you. I
wouldn't want you thinking I expected anything for
paying your fine and putting you to work.'

A new look entered her eyes. It was as equally hard to
comprehend as the last. 'And you think I'm the kind of
girl who would *thank you* with my favors?'

'No! Of course not. I wanted you to know that you

. . . that you're not indentured to me in any other way. I was. . . .' he was lost. 'I mean, I didn't want to. . . .'

Allyson finally raised her hand and put a finger up to his lips. He stopped trying to remove his feet from his mouth, but the distinct taste of shoe leather lingered.

'I don't think you are any better at romance than I am, Yancy.'

'True enough,' he admitted. 'I've not had much practice.'

'You can relax. You didn't take advantage of me,' she said quietly. Her complexion darkened a shade. 'If you noticed, I kissed you back.'

He swallowed hard, but the tang of his shoes remained. 'I would never force my attentions on you. I'm not that kind of guy.'

She finally smiled and allowed him to squirm off the hook. 'I know what kind of guy you are, Yancy. You are the first man I've cared about since my father was killed.' The smile faded. 'However, I don't think of you in a fatherly light.'

That put some fire back into Yancy. He reached out for her, thinking he would use the sweetness of her lips to rid himself of the taste of shoe leather. However, Allyson deftly ducked away.

'You'd best get started.' She was businesslike. 'Kara and I will be waiting for you to return. I'll tend the store as best I can until then.'

'But you said that. . . .'

She stepped past him and opened the door. 'Goodbye, Yancy. Please be careful and hurry back.'

He frowned and shuffled past her. One little kiss was

all he was going to get. It was kind of like a single lick of ice cream or a solitary taste of a sugar stick. His appetite was alive; he craved more, and suddenly the candy and ice cream had been snatched out of his reach.

'Give a fellow apoplexy doing that,' he muttered aloud. 'What kind of damage does that do to a man's system? Turn up the heat and douse the fire at the same time. It could ruin a man for life!'

'Are you saying something?' Allyson pretended not to hear his words clearly enough to understand.

'Yeah,' he paused. 'I'm saying for you to be careful and mind the store.'

'We'll be just fine.'

He offered nothing else, but trudged up the street. Until that encounter, he had no idea the number of different sensations a woman could cause in a man – all at the same time. Raised to a state of euphoria, crushed beneath the weight of rejection, riding high one minute and shot out of the saddle the next. He had to wonder if God really intended for man to understand the female of the species. Somehow, he doubted it.

Eight

Yancy pulled up the collar of his jacket and tipped his hat down against the cold wind. The snow was gone, but summer was still some weeks away. The horse Wade had provided was a solid animal. It had been a quick trip and he was making good time.

He thought about the saddlebags and the leaflets inside. It would be a grim reminder as to what Hilton Conway stood for. Wade and John had listed items that Yancy had not even known about. Once the people saw the number of atrocities in black and white, they would be forced to vote him out of office.

Thinking along those lines, he knew about the young couple losing the bakery, about Curly and the death of Cal Smith. He had not been aware of the fact that seven different businesses had closed in the past two years, all due to the burden of taxes. He had not known about the traveling drummer who had been hanged without a trial. There had been other things too: the beating of several people, the shooting of another, the death of a drunk who made an off-color comment to Mrs Conway. It all mounted up.

Examining the landmarks, he figured he was about thirty miles from Pine Junction. He thought back to the last time he had made this trip, when he had found the Conestoga wagon and discovered Kara and her parents. It had been his good fortune to happen along before the cold and hunger took Kara's life. He hoped one day she would. . . .

Something hit him hard in the chest, like a hammer swung with incredible force. It knocked him out of the saddle. His horse jumped at the echo of a rifle shot and bolted off in a dead run.

Yancy was lying on his back, but he had not felt himself hit the ground. He stared at the sky, trying to get his mind to function, unable to draw a breath. He thought for a moment that he had been struck by lightning, then he heard the fading steps of a horse.

Motionless, his first sensation was that there was a wetness inside his shirt. A numbness spread all across his chest, but he finally sucked in enough air to breathe. A stark realization entered his head. He'd been shot!

Twisting his neck, he searched the surrounding area. He could not see or hear anyone. His head was spinning, but he managed to get his gun out. Using his elbows and digging in his heels he slowly began to inch into the brush, seeking cover.

He was sweating from the effort, holding his gun ready, uncertain as to how bad he was hit. He grunted from the pain, put his free hand over his chest and rose to a sitting position so that he could take a look around.

His horse had run about a hundred feet and was standing with her ears perked. Yancy followed the direction she was looking and saw a distant rider, too far away to identify. He was heading towards Pine Junction, which meant he didn't intend to check on the condition of the man he had ambushed.

Falling back to a prone position, Yancy shoved his gun into its holster. Then he opened his coat and unbuttoned his shirt. There was a puncture on the left side of his chest, but it was high enough that it had missed his lung. He felt around but found no exit wound, so he guessed the bullet had struck his shoulder blade or other major bone. It was still in his body. He stuffed his bandanna into the wound to stop the bleeding.

His mind was racing. He knew that his chance for survival, alone, without treatment, was slim. He had to catch the horse and make it to Pine Junction. He could stop the bleeding externally, but his body was not going to appreciate carrying a piece of lead about. If he did not get help, he would very probably die.

Allyson stood at the window and kept watch. She looked upward at the dark sky. Yancy should have been back before the sun went down. He had said four days, and a fifth was about to pass. Something was dreadfully wrong.

'Isn't daddy going to be home for supper?' Kara spoke up to her back.

'I hoped he would be here by now. Maybe it got too dark and he had to spend another night on the trail.' She hid her worry and smiled over her shoulder at the little girl. 'You remember how it was traveling? It's very hard to see after dark.'

'Yep, I didn't like that none. It was always cold and we didn't have nothing to eat.' She let out a pronounced sigh. 'You think daddy has enough to eat?'

'I'm sure he's all right.' She forced conviction into her words. 'If he isn't here by early tomorrow, I'll ask John or Wade to go look for him.'

Allyson served up the meager supper, but she had no appetite. She toyed with her food and took only a few small bites. She mustered a false bravado for Kara's sake, but inside she was worried sick.

What if something dreadful had happened to Yancey? What if he simply never returned? Her sixty days would soon be paid for, but then what? She could not adopt Kara on her own. She had no lawful right to take over the store and run it in Yancy's absence. Besides which, she had not learned the trade well enough to keep it open. Without Yancy, all three of them would be lost and alone.

Making a hasty decision, she got up from the table. 'Give the scraps to Bunny. I'm going to speak to Wade. I won't be gone very long.'

'OK, Allie. You want me to tell daddy where you are, if he comes?'

'Yes. If he shows up, send him to fetch me.'

Allyson wrapped her jacket about her shoulders and hurried into the dark. She knew it was not a good idea to visit Wade's High Card Saloon, but her worry was stronger than her fear of what people might say. After all, she had been going to saloons for the entire two years she was with Curly and no one ever rebuked her for it.

The King's Full was brightly lit, and music blared from the piano Conway had brought into Pine Junction. There was the sound of a woman's laughter, high-pitched and harsh. Allyson gave that place a wide berth.

The High Card was practically deserted. There was a card game at one table and a couple of cowboys were drinking at the bar. Pausing before the bat-wing doors, Wade was not in sight. Allyson took a deep breath and entered the bar room.

'Hey! We don't allow no. . . .' The bartender had started to speak, but he recognized Allyson. 'Oh, it's you.' He frowned. 'You want a chocolate drink this late at night?'

She ignored the stares from the other men in the room and turned her attention to the heavy-set man behind the counter. 'No, I must see Mr Wade. Is he upstairs?'

A man rose from the card table. Until that moment, Allyson had not recognized Leroy Queen. He was unsteady, as if he had been drinking too much. The star pinned to his shirt was hanging crooked, and so too was the twisted smile on his lips.

'You want to go upstairs with a man, honey, you ought to be spending your time over at Hilton's saloon.'

She took a step back, ready to bolt from the room. 'I need to speak to Mr Wade.'

Queen looked her over slowly, his gaze traveling up and down like a man judging a horse. When the red-rimmed eyes rested on her face, she cringed inwardly.

'You've been getting pretty uppity, ever since you hitched your buggy to that saddle-maker's team. Maybe you do more than keep his house and tend his kid.'

Allyson turned to the bartender for help, but he hurried to draw a beer for one of the cowboys. They were both looking her over with an odd curiosity.

'You boys remember Curly Muldoon?' Queen asked the pair. At their nod, he pointed an unsteady finger at Allyson. 'Well, this is his squaw.'

'Sure,' one of them replied, 'the half-breed gal he always dragged around with him. I wondered what happened to her.'

'I was not his squaw!' Allyson snapped. 'He was my guardian.'

Queen guffawed loudly. 'Sure . . . he was your guardian. What was I thinking?' Then he put an ugly sneer on his face. 'You boys ever wonder what it would be like to kiss a squaw?'

Allyson knew liquor often destroyed a man's good sense. The cowboys were looking for some fun and Queen was looking for trouble. She backed towards the door, but suddenly another man blocked her way – the weasel of Pine Junction, Zip Lovendaul.

'Say, Queeny!' he grinned broadly. 'What've you got here, some sport for us?'

'She came looking for Wade.'

He laughed. 'Now ain't that a kick in the chops? I been looking for Wade all afternoon myself. It seems he sprouted wings and flew the coop.'

Allyson was trapped between the two men. The cowboys were both drunk and had silly grins pasted on their mugs. The other men at the card table were enjoying the taunting. It left her with only her own wits to escape the explosive situation.

'Perhaps you could tell Hilton Conway I'd like to speak to him.'

The bluff did not fool Queen. 'You dress like a white woman and stick your nose in the air, but you're a half-breed. You got no business with Mr Conway.'

'You want to talk to someone, 'breed,' Lovendaul hissed from behind her, 'You can talk to me and Queeny.'

Allyson took a step to her right and then sprang to the left. She tried to dart past Lovendaul, but he was too quick. His hand caught hold of her arm.

She was jerked around and into his grasp. With his force propelling her, she swung at his face with a tightly-balled fist. The leering smile was squashed with the impact of her punch.

Lovendaul howled in pain and released her, but Queen was there to grab her.

'Ye-hah!' he yelled, pinning her arms at her sides. 'Talk about a wildcat!'

Lovendaul put a hand to his mouth and found blood coming from a cut on his lip. 'Look what that 'breed did!' he cried. 'She split my lip open!'

'Reckon we'd best take her to jail!' Queen declared.

'Assaulting an officer of the law is a lock-up offence. We'll toss her in a cell for the night.'

'The hell with that idea!' Lovendaul bellowed. 'I'm going to smash her face in!'

'Better not,' the bartender spoke up. 'You remember what that saddle-maker done to you before.'

Lovendaul glowered over at him. 'Yeah, well that tough guy ain't going to be mixing it up with anyone again. We've seen the last of him.'

Even as she feared for her own safety, Allyson was crushed by the man's words. He had spoken with a grim finality. 'What have you done to him?' she cried. 'What have you done to Yancy Nodean?'

But Lovendaul nodded to Queen. 'Take her to the jail.' He spat blood on to the floor of the saloon. 'The spitfire is going to pay for hitting me.'

Allyson searched the faces of the other men in the room, but they were cowed by the two lawmen. She knew she should have gone over and fetched John. He could have rounded up Wade and avoided trouble.

Ice crystals encrusted her heart. She struggled in Queen's grasp, but his fingers taloned into her arms. He was more than a match for her. A vast emptiness flooded her being. She was jerked about and shoved out into the night. Queen had a firm hold on her and Lovendaul was right behind them. Allison was filled with the fear of helplessness. The deputies could do whatever they pleased – there was no one to help her.

The cold night air penetrated Yancy's clothing, but he was still burning up with fever. He sat on the ground and tried to think rationally. The blood-red mare was gone. He was a stranger to her, so the animal had spooked and run off. 'Stupid blasted horse,' he muttered.

The night air carried the sounds of something moving, but Yancy ignored it. He knew there were only a few coyotes in that part of Wyoming. Were it possibly a bear or puma, he would have been worried. A lone coyote or two would not attack a man . . . at least, not until he was near death.

'I ain't dead yet,' he snarled, staring into the blackness of night. 'You might as well look for a fawn or dying antelope! I'll be as tough-eating as tree bark.'

Yancy had become confused about which way to go. He remained sitting, conserving strength. At daylight, he would get his bearings and strike out for Pine Junction again.

The pounding in his skull was like a sixteen-pound hammer striking an anvil. The fire of fever raged in his body. He closed his eyes against the pain and lowered his head. He groped for rational thoughts and searched for something to which he could cling.

Images floated in assorted bits and pieces across his mind's eye. When he pictured Kara and Allyson, he concentrated on their faces. With all of his might, he forced his brain to focus only on the two of them. They were the reason he would survive being shot. He could not let them down.

'So here you are!' a voice sliced through his thoughts like a sharp blade. 'You're off of the trail by half a mile!'

Yancy had to blink several times to get the fog out of

his eyes. He discovered Everett Wade standing over him. 'Wha. . . ? How'd you manage to find me?'

'The horse came back without you. I've been riding circles for the past four hours. You're a hard man to find.'

'I've been right here,' Yancy replied wearily. 'If you'd have looked where I was at to start with, you'd have found me right off.'

Wade placed his hand on Yancy's brow. Funny, his hand was cold to the touch.

'I'll get a fire going. Then I'll have a look at how badly you've been hit.'

'Why the fire? It ain't a bit cold.'

'I figured to roast your gizzard for the trouble you've caused me.'

'Whatever you say, Wade.'

The man started a fire and then he helped Yancy stretch out on a blanket. He pulled back his shirt to examine the wound. A few prods ignited searing pains all through Yancy's chest.

'I'm a little rusty at this,' he said, placing the blade of a jack-knife so it was in the fire. 'Been some time since I removed a bullet.'

'You?' Yancy was not that far from reality. 'You're going to remove the slug?'

'Unless you want to try and do it yourself.'

'Can't we get a real doctor?'

'Ain't a real doctor this side of the fort. I doubt you'd make it that far.'

'I'm willing to give it a try.'

But Wade shook his head. 'I done my share of helping during the war, Nodean. I was attached to a medical unit.' He grinned. 'Watched so many men die I took up selling rot-gut for a living.'

'Maybe the bullet don't need to come out,' Yancy suggested. 'Maybe it'll heal by itself.'

Wade was not of a mind to be swayed. 'Don't be such a sissy, Nodean. I'll get the bullet out.' He grinned again. 'Might take me three or four tries, but I'll get it out.'

'I should have crawled under a rock, so you couldn't find me.'

'Too late for hiding, Nodean. Like I said, you've nothing to worry about. I practise my craft every year.' He grinned, 'I carve the Thanksgiving turkey.'

'That makes me feel a whole lot better about the idea.'

Wade held out a bottle of whiskey. 'I even brought along some painkiller.'

Yancy took a swallow of the foul-tasting liquid and let it burn down his throat. 'Holy smoke! If you don't kill me with the knife, this stuff will finish the job.'

'Drink up, Nodean. The blade is about ready.'

'I thought you heated the blade to sear closed a wound?'

'Sure, but I have to burn the blade clean too. You know, I can't remember what I used that knife on last. Might have skinned a rabbit or cut up some venison. Not to worry, I'll let it cool a bit before I go probing for the bullet.'

Yancy groaned and took another long pull from the bottle. He hoped the whiskey was enough to deaden his senses. If not, his cries of pain were going to raise the dead.

Allyson bit back the plea for mercy which rose to her lips. She was tied to and facing the cell bars. Lovendaul had torn off her jacket and was standing right against her, hissing his words over her shoulder.

'I'm going to teach you a lesson, 'breed!' He uttered a guttural laugh, 'I'll bet you remember how the Indians keep their squaws in line?'

'I'm not a squaw,' she told him. 'My mother was Mexican.'

He chortled again. 'Indian – Mexican, it don't make no difference to me.'

With a violent jerk, he ripped the rear of her dress open to expose her back. She stifled a cry, knowing her screams would only add to Lovendaul's satisfaction.

'I've got a nice leather belt here, 'breed. I'm going to use it on that pretty bare skin of yours. I'll bet you scream your head off the first time it touches you.'

'Give her a swat, Zip. I'll wager you two bucks she don't cry out right off.'

'Hear that, 'breed? You cry out with the first whack and I win. If you don't, I'm out two bucks.' Lovendaul pushed his face up close to her cheek. 'I won't like losing.'

Allyson laced her fingers about the bars and clung to them. She set her teeth and closed her eyes tightly. Having never been beaten with a strap, she had no idea what her reaction would be to the pain.

The swish of the belt was audible until it smacked

Allyson's bare flesh. The searing sting ignited fire all down her back and across her shoulders. She sharply sucked in her breath, arched her back and moaned against the pain.

'Ye-hah! What'd I tell you, Zip? Nothing but a whimper! She didn't cry out.'

Lovendaul swore vehemently. 'You filthy half-breed witch! You done cost me two bucks!'

Allyson braced herself against the next onslaught, but it did not come. The door to the jail opened and someone entered the room.

'What's going on here, Lovendaul?'

Allyson risked a glance over her shoulder. The new arrival was Chaw Benedict. He was scowling at the other two deputies.

'The gal hit Zip in the mouth,' Queen explained. 'We was teaching her a lesson.'

'You got no right to butt in, Chaw.' Lovendaul was hostile. 'That is, unless you want a piece of the action. We've got a bet on how long it will be before she cries out.'

'Turn her loose!' Chaw demanded.

'Hey, big man!' Zip sneered. 'You don't give no orders here!'

Chaw's gun appeared with such speed it might have materialized out of thin air. He had both men covered before they even knew he intended to draw.

'Whoa there, Chaw!' Queen backed away at once. 'Don't get testy. We were just having some fun.'

'I said to turn her loose!'

'Sure, sure, I'm doing it.' Queen was quick to work the

ropes loose with his fingers. Lovendaul remained frozen in place, looking into the muzzle of the man's gun.

'You're supposed to be one of us,' he said, after the shock had worn off. 'What's the matter with you?'

'I wear a badge, Lovendaul. I believe in what it stands for.'

'Since when?'

'Since my eyes opened to what you scum are all about. I've stood by and let you clowns do whatever you wanted to intimidate the people. I let it ride, concerned only about making high wages. Well, I'm through with all of you. When the election is over – win or lose – I'm turning in my star.'

'Can't be too soon to suit me,' Queen said, his teeth anchored. 'I never figured you would pull iron on us.'

Chaw picked up Allyson's coat with his left hand and passed it to her. 'I'll see you home, ma'am. I'm right sorry I didn't get here sooner.'

She shrugged into the coat and quickly moved over behind the man. He holstered his gun and continued to glare at the two other deputies.

'If you've an idea to test me with a gun, I'm waiting,' he tossed out the threat. 'One or both of you at the same time – makes no never-mind to me.'

But neither of the men picked up the gauntlet. He backed out the door, without turning his back to them. Then he took hold of Allyson's wrist and started off towards Yancy's house.

'That was a fool stunt, Miss Jenkins. You ought to know better than to enter a saloon. Lucky for you the bartender was concerned about you.'

'I was looking for Wade. Yancy . . . Mr Nodean has not returned.'

'Can't do much in the middle of the night,' he answered. 'Besides which, Wade is already out looking for your feller. He left late this afternoon.'

'How do you know so much?'

He lifted a shoulder indifferently. 'I keep an eye on what goes on.'

'I . . . I don't know how to thank you for coming to my rescue. If you hadn't arrived when you did, I. . . .'

'The law is not exclusively on Hilton Conway's side,' he cut her short. 'You don't owe me anything. I was doing my job.'

'Thank you all the same.'

He smiled at her. 'When you see your guy, tell him that he owes me one.'

Nine

Consciousness returned slowly to Yancy. He was tired and lethargic. The dull pounding in his skull reminded him that drinking hard liquor was not an intelligent thing to do. There was another throbbing along his left side and shoulder. The area was tightly bound with a bandage, but each movement and breath sent spasms of pain lancing through him.

'About time you decided to wake up,' Wade was gruff. 'You ought to show some consideration for your doctor.'

'My mouth tastes like someone ran a herd of sheep across my tongue. That rot-gut whiskey is enough to make a man take up sobriety.'

'Bite your tongue,' Wade scolded him. 'Them there is bitter, hateful words. If people got to thinking being sober was what life is all about, I'd be out of business.'

'Well, far be it from me to ruin your life, Wade. But I'd just as soon live without booze, gambling and the night-life.'

'Killjoy!' Wade grunted. 'You make me sorry I fretted over you all night.'

Yancy's head began to clear. 'How did you find me?'

'I told you last night.'

'Yeah, but I wasn't thinking too straight.'

'Never mind about trifles. Did you see who bush-whacked you?'

'Only a rider in the distance. I wouldn't be able to point a finger at him.'

'Lovendaul has been out of town since you left. I'd bet all of the whiskey in my saloon that he pulled the trigger.'

'It would be about his style.'

'We've got to get you back into town quietly. You can lay low for a time, until you get your strength back.'

'The election won't wait for me.'

'It isn't for a few days yet. You need to take time to heal up proper.'

'Speaking of the wound, the shoulder feels pretty good. You must have gotten the bullet out without much trouble.'

Wade shrugged. 'It wasn't much of a challenge. I dug around until I hit bone and then worked the slug back out the wound. I could have done it in my sleep.'

'Did I set up a holler?'

'Wailed like a banshee in a bear trap,' Wade said. 'I seen two coyotes run past at first light and both of them had cotton in their ears.'

'You ought to consider telling your stories to customers, Wade. You'd draw a bigger crowd than the dancing girls that Hilton brought in.'

'Afraid not, Nodean. They've got pretty legs. Me, I got legs like a chicken. It would be no contest.'

Yancy took a deep breath and winced from the pain. He clenched his teeth against the discomfort. 'We going to make it to Pine Junction today?'

'Not if you keep jawing,' Wade replied. 'I've burned some beans and bacon for breakfast. That'll give you more incentive not to quit on me. I cook like you sing.'

'How do you know how I sing?'

'I told you about the coyotes,' he said. 'With a voice like yours, you ought to learn sign language and practise it faithfully.'

'You're a real pal, Wade.'

He chuckled. 'At least we agree on that much.'

'Soon as we get back to town, I want you to send off a telegram for me. Man's name is Konrad Ellington.'

'Sure thing,' with another grin, 'if you live long enough to get back to town.'

Jay Slone stood with his hat in his hands, turning it slowly, studying the band as if he had never really looked at it before.

'I'm sure you've seen the handbills spread all over town?' Hilton was fuming. 'It makes us look like the biggest crooks in the country!'

'I don't know where they came from. Lovendaul said he found Nodean dead on the trail. Ain't no way them print-outs should have ever reached here.'

Hilton threw his hands in the air. 'Each of those notices is a nail in our coffin, Slone. We won't carry the votes to win.'

'We still have a couple days.'

'To do what? The notice says we set fire to Cal's tavern!'

'Actually, it was Queen.'

Hilton was devastated. 'What's the matter with you, Slone? We never discussed burning him out.'

Slone rotated the hat once more. 'We have to stay in control, Hilton. I've done what had to be done.'

Hilton suddenly felt very old. 'It's over, Slone. When I lose the job of mayor, we lose the chance to ever bring the railroad to Pine Junction! We're done!'

'We could force Tompkins to withdraw. He's got a wife and store to think about.'

'One threat and he'll be on Judge Mantie's doorstep. We'd have the army down here before you could clean the wax out of your ears.'

'You want to give up without a fight?'

'What about your own men? I heard some of your boys had a falling out with Chaw Benedict? Jarvis told me he heard you fired him.'

'Chaw was taking his badge too seriously. That 'breed, the one who cut me, was about to get her due. She clouted Lovendaul right in the puss. His lip is swollen about twice its normal size today. Anyway, Zip hauled her to jail and was going to teach her a lesson, when Chaw showed up.'

'So Chaw and Queen had words?'

'Chaw drew down on them both – Zip and Leroy. He took the girl home and threatened to kill them if they tried to stop him.'

'It's all falling apart, Slone. By firing the man, it puts

him on the other side and makes us look all the more guilty.'

'I didn't have any options. Zip and Leroy are loyal to our cause and will carry out orders without question. I couldn't very well side with Chaw and lose their support.'

'It's water over the dam now,' Hilton said. 'We're out of options. Is there any way we can rig the ballots in our favor?'

'The way Mantie explained it, he is going to personally oversee the voting. He will check each person's name off of the town register and watch them put their vote into the box. Once time has expired or everyone has voted, he'll do the count himself.'

'And I suppose he has a list of the voters who are eligible?'

'Tompkins and I are to compare lists in front of the judge. That means he can challenge anyone and I can do the same. The judge will rule on who can or can't vote.'

'Think Tompkins will challenge our employees?'

'I doubt it. He thinks he can win without their support.'

Flora entered the room, dressed in a blue velvet gown. It was fashionably decorated at the flounce with a row of black ribbons. The bodice was buttoned up the front and cut low on the shoulders. The exposed portion of her skin appeared as soft as the breast of a dove. Hilton expected she had heard their words from the adjacent room.

'Would you care for a glass of sherry, Hilly?' Her voice was as smooth as silk. 'Perhaps for your guest too?'

'No, thank you, Mrs Conway,' Slone replied. to the offer. 'I've got to get back to work.'

'Hilly?'

He had to force his voice to function. She was such a magnificent woman, so beautiful that it often took away his power of speech. 'Thank you, Flora, but we are fine.'

'Well,' she cocked her head to one side and smiled sweetly. 'I won't take any more of your time. I am going for my morning walk with Jarvis.'

'That's fine, Flora, honey.'

She tipped her head ever so slightly in farewell, then glided out of the room.

Hilton was overcome with a new energy. Each time he was close to Flora, he knew she was the only really important thing in his life.

He was suddenly irate, fearful he would lose Flora. 'There's got to be a way to win the election. We've got a fortune in coal here. We can be rich men.' He pounded his fist into an open palm. 'We can't give it all up!'

There was a long silence, before Slone finally spoke. 'John isn't anything without Yancy Nodean backing his play.' At Hilton's eager look, he continued. 'If the saddle-maker is out of the picture – and Lovendaul says he is – that makes his kid an orphan again.'

'Yes, so what?'

'Even if he shows up, I did some checking on the man. It seems he was sentenced to prison a few months back – to serve eight years.'

Hilton frowned at the news. 'What's he doing running free then?'

'I don't know, but it gives us leverage. We can use his kid to control his supporters. We grab the kid, all legal like, and make it known that she is being held in temporary custody until after the election. We let there be a whisper around town that, if we don't win, he never gets her back again.'

'It'll do no good, once people learn Nodean is dead.'

'We'll keep that quiet. Lovendaul hasn't told anyone but me. There will be some of John's backers who will vote our way to prevent the little girl from being taken away from Nodean.'

'What if someone goes to Mantie or the army?'

'We can defend our actions. The kid is either an orphan or she was adopted by an escaped convict – right?' He grinned. 'Well, we are doing our civic duty to take her away from Nodean.'

'I don't like the idea of using a little kid for leverage.'

'We talk to the 'breed too,' Slone suggested. 'After all, she still owes some of her sixty days jail time. She can co-operate or spend the rest of her sentence behind bars. I can tell you, she won't want to go to jail again.'

Hilton ran his hand over his brow. He did not relish the idea of snatching up some kid. People would take a real dim view of using children as pawns in a power struggle. But Slone had the perfect answer to that. They were only watching after the little waif. She was an orphan. Who would resent them for taking her away from a half-breed wildcat like Allyson?

'Do what you think is best, Slone,' he said, at length. 'The only thing important to us at the moment is winning the election. We can make everything right after we secure our positions.'

'Leave it to me, boss. With that little joker in our hand, no one will dare cross us.'

Yancy was on the bed, propped up with pillows, when Allyson entered the room. She had tears in her eyes.

'I thought Wade told you to keep your distance until election day?' He tried to scold her, but his heart was glad to see her again.

Allyson came to the edge of the bed and dropped down to her knees. She buried her face in his chest, carefully putting her arms around him.

'I couldn't stay away. Something . . . something has happened that. . . .'

A scalding pain splashed up his shoulder and down into his chest, but he used his good hand to lift her chin. 'What? Tell me what!'

Allyson sniffed back the impending flow of tears. Her face showed a forlorn expression. It was enough to flood Yancy with apprehension and a sudden fear.

'Slone and his men came to the house. They took Kara and her dog. Lovendaul said you were an escaped convict from prison. They said Kara would have to stay with them until after the election.'

Yancy felt a new sensation, the fires of anger. He had some of his strength back, but he was still weak from his wound.

'What else has happened in the past couple of days?'

'I suppose Wade told you about Chaw getting fired for helping me?'

He squeezed her hand gently. 'Yes. I owe him a debt for that.'

'Well, Slone's cousin from the saloon is wearing a badge now. His name is Clayton.'

'That makes four of them again.'

'They took Kara to the jail. I'm sure they plan to use her as leverage to get people to vote for them. Everything will appear legal, but her very life is in danger.'

'Not if I set the record straight,' he said, firmly. 'They can't hold my daughter, once I prove why I'm in Pine Junction.'

'Slone will be forced to kill you!'

Yancy ignored the threat. He pushed her back from the bed, swung his legs over the side and gingerly pushed himself upright with his right hand.

'Help me with my boots,' he said.

'You can't be up and around, Yancy! You can't even stand up!'

He put a steady look on her. 'Those buzzards are not taking my daughter away from me, Allyson. I've got to get her back.'

She saw the resolve in his face and quickly helped him to get dressed.

When Yancy rose to his feet, the room spun before his eyes. He fought the swirling motion until it settled down, before he took a deep breath and ventured a step.

He was not steady, but he seemed to grow stronger

and more assured with each passing minute. By the time Allyson helped to strap on his gun, he had a clear head. Only the pain of movement reminded him of his gunshot wound. He would have to baby his left side and not do anything sudden . . . like drawing or shooting his gun.

'Get word to Ward that I'm going to visit John. Have him meet me there. If I get enough people backing my play, Slone won't dare try anything.'

'All right, Yancy.' Her voice was soft.

He paused for a moment, drinking in her subtle beauty. Impulsively, he reached out and drew her to him. She did not resist his advance, coming into his arms willingly. Allyson kissed him and stood encircled in his arms for a few precious moments. Then she broke away and hurried from the room.

Yancy pulled his gun and checked the loads. He had been in Wade's storehouse for only a single day and night. He knew his strength would not last. The action he took would have to be quick and decisive. Once he got Kara back, he could go to his own house. There would be no surprises on election day.

Zip Lovendaul threw open the door of the marshal's office. He had a panicked look on his face.

'What's up?' Queen asked. 'You look like you just spotted a ghost.'

'That's exactly what I done! I spotted me a real live, walking, talking ghost! And he's a-coming this way!'

Queen shot a quick glance at the little moppet in the

corner of the room. She and the shaggy puppy on her lap had not moved from the spot in over an hour.

'Speak sense, Lovendaul. What are you talking about?'

'Nodean is headed this way! He's got John, Wade and Chaw Benedict at his side!'

'Daddy?' Kara cried. 'Daddy is coming to get me!'

'Stay put!' Queen snarled at her.

But she was on her feet. She ran for the door, with the pup hot on her heels.

'Daddy!' she shouted. 'I'm in here, Daddy!'

'Grab that kid!' Queen swore and reached for Kara.

She ducked and tried to squirm past Lovendaul. He caught hold of her jacket and jerked her back into the office. She screamed and the dog came to her defence, sinking his teeth into Lovendaul's ankle.

'Ye-ow!' He let out a howl and kicked the dog across the room. It hit the wall hard and lay dazed.

'Bunny!' Kara shrieked and bolted from his grasp, rushing to her puppy. She began sobbing and cuddling the tiny dog in her arms.

'What'll we do?' Lovendaul was in a panic.

'Where is Slone?'

'He and his cousin went up to talk to Hilton. We're on our own.'

Queen put his hand on his gun, but shook his head. 'We can't take Chaw and the others in a fight. Let's get out of here and go warn Slone what has happened.'

The two of them hurried out the rear of the jail, leaving Kara on the floor crying over her injured dog.

That was how Yancy found his daughter. Her grief over the pup outweighed her relief at seeing him again.

'They kicked Bunny!' she said, tearfully. 'They've killed my little dog!'

Yancy knelt down next to her and took Bunny from her arms. The pup was dazed and unsteady, but was recovering quickly. When he put him on the floor, Bunny shook his head and then his entire body, as if removing the effects of the blow.

'He protected me, Daddy,' Kara said, joyfully sweeping the pup into her arms once more. 'He was a real tiger!'

'Where did the deputies go?'

'Out the back door. One man said they were going to find Mr Slone. Bunny and you scared them away.'

'What now?' Chaw spoke up. 'Do we wait for the judge?'

'I say we put those murdering crooks behind bars!' John growled the words. 'They ambushed Nodean and kidnapped his daughter. To my way of thinking, they'll do anything to win this election. The longer we let them run loose, the more chance they'll kill someone else.'

Chaw turned his attention to Wade. 'What's your vote?'

'I'll go along with John. We can't risk letting them get organized again. There isn't time to call in the army.'

'And you, Nodean?'

Yancy took a long look at his little girl. Allyson had followed after the four men. There was something supportive about her expression. He knew she was leaving the decision up to him.

'Slone killed Cal Smith.' Wade outlined the deeds. 'It's for certain you were waylaid by Zip Lovendaul. Leroy Queen probably had a hand in setting fire to Cal's place, and he has done his share of other dirty jobs. As for Hilton Conway, he's the man giving orders.'

'Then we need to put them all behind bars,' Yancy said. 'And that won't be easy.'

John cleared his throat and took the floor. 'As prospective mayor, I hereby appoint Chaw Benedict the new marshal of Pine Junction. I'll be accountable for any actions taken today.'

Chaw went over to the desk and opened a drawer. He removed several tin stars.

'As my first act as the new marshal, I'm swearing you boys in as deputies. If you can think of anyone else who will side with us, give them one of these too. We'll meet at the livery in fifteen minutes.'

'Why the livery?'

'Nodean's freight wagon has thick side-boards for hauling ore. It ought to be enough to stop a bullet from most handguns. We'll need cover on our approach, just in case they start throwing lead.'

Yancy gave a nod. 'My team of horses are fat and sassy from not doing a lick of work all winter. I guess they can use some exercise at that.'

'We've got company!' Wade spoke up, looking out into the street. 'Anyone know this guy?'

Yancy used some of his valuable energy to step to the window. It was worth the effort and the pain. 'It's Konrad Ellington!'

'And who might he be?' John asked.

'Our leader,' Yancy told them as a group.

Konrad dusted off his hat, automatically removed the thong which held his Colt firmly in its holster, and stepped up on to the porch.

'Come on in, Marshal,' Yancy greeted him. 'Glad you could make it.'

Konrad looked around at the men's faces, then paused to put a curious look on Chaw Benedict. 'I've seen you before.' He stated it as a fact. 'You're wanted for questioning concerning a cattle rustling operation.'

Chaw frowned. 'You've got a memory like a steel trap, Marshal. You only seen me the one time, when I rode into town with my wounded brother.'

'I recall he died of the injury, before we had a chance to deal out real justice.'

Chaw's shoulders sagged. 'What can I say? I always did what my brother told me to do. He and my uncle stole cattle for a living and they needed someone to mind the horses and do the camp chores. I rode with them on a couple raids, before we were ambushed.'

Konrad gave his head a nod. 'It's been three years,' he said. 'You been keeping your nose clean since then?'

'Until I got mixed up here in Pine Junction. I haven't broke any laws, but I've certainly bent a few.'

'I'll vouch for him,' John said. 'He's an honest and decent man.'

'Saved my future wife from taking a severe beating with a strap,' Yancy spoke up as well. 'I'd trust him with my life.'

Konrad looked around and saw all were in agreement. 'If you want to keep wearing that badge and do a good job here, Chaw, I'll have that old Wanted poster cleared up for you.'

'Anything you say, Marshal.'

'What's the plan?' Konrad asked. 'It looks as if you're getting ready for a war.'

'We hope not, but the time has come to put a few men behind bars.'

Konrad looked at Yancy. 'You got the proof?'

'Lovendaul ambushed me. We know these guys set fire to a place in town and they've used town funds to pay for their mining operation and also to hire people to work at the saloon. Slone has killed two people – and one of them only had a knife on him.'

'Sounds a little thin for murder.'

'I figure he was the one who ordered my death.'

'Let's go talk to these fellows and see what they've got to say for themselves.'

The men left the office, except for Yancy. He waited until Allyson had hold of Kara's hand. Bunny was tucked in tightly under her other arm.

'Be careful, Yancy,' Allyson said. 'When I thought you were dead, it about killed me inside. I . . . I wouldn't want to feel that much pain again.'

He leaned over and kissed her lightly.

'What about me?' Kara asked. 'Allie didn't feel no badder than me.'

Yancy kissed her on the cheek as well. 'I love you both.'

Kara beamed. 'Do that mean Allie is gonna be my new mommy?'

'I don't know if she would want to tackle such a job,'

he replied. 'She has her own life to lead. We'll have to see about that after this little chore.'

Allyson was steadfast. 'You keep your mind on your business, Yancy Nodean. If you get yourself killed, I won't soon forgive you.'

Yancy felt his chest expand. It was a wonder the buttons did not pop from his shirt. He was lost in her eyes for a long moment. 'Take Kara home, darlin'. This won't take long.'

She displayed a warm smile. 'Whatever you say, Yancy. We'll be waiting for you.'

He watched the two of them walk towards their house. What a lucky man he was. Who could ask for more than being free and having the love of two beautiful girls? He was surely blessed.

Then he removed his gun and checked the loads again. Only one obstacle remained between him and a life of happiness and joy – Hilton Conway and his men.

Ten

'We're out of time!' Jay Slone snarled the words at Hilton. 'With Nodean having his kid back and those circulars all over town, we haven't got a chance of winning the election!'

'I thought you said Nodean was dead?' Hilton looked at Lovendaul. 'You claimed someone had killed him on the trail? You supposedly buried him!'

'I hit him square in the brisket,' Lovendaul whined. 'Knocked him out of the saddle and he landed like a sack of grain. The man must have the lives of a cat.'

'You're a boneheaded fool!' Hilton fumed. 'I never ordered anyone killed!'

Lovendaul grew flushed with anger. 'Hey! Slone says to keep an eye on him. He went and talked to them rail-road people. Then he had them signs made up so we would look bad and lose the election. I figured we ought to put him out of *our* misery.'

Slone moved in between the two men. He held up his hands to silence both sides. 'The question is, boss, what do we do now?'

150

'You've gone too far, Slone. I didn't know you were going to burn Calvin's place down until it was ashes. You said there would be no killing, yet Calvin died that very night. Now, I learn that you ordered Lovendaul to kill Nodean. This isn't the way our plan was supposed to work!'

'You wanted to stay in power,' Slone argued. 'How did you expect me to accomplish that feat – with magic?'

'There's a wagon coming,' Queen interrupted from the front window of the house. 'I count three men in the wagon and a couple more on foot. One of them is a big fellow with a badge.'

'Hate to be a turn-tail-and-run sort, Jay.' Clayton Slone was grave. 'But you didn't tell me you were going to start a war. I don't intend to get killed in Pine Junction.'

'You want out, you're out.' Jay's words were curt.

'No hard feelings.' Clayton removed his badge and tossed it to Jay. Then he went quickly out the front door and hurried away. After the door closed, the four men were alone in the room.

'This don't look good.' Queen was watching the front of the house. 'They turned the wagon sideways. They are all fanned out and have taken cover.'

'Hilly?' The woman's voice turned all heads towards Flora.

'Yes, Flora, honey?'

'What's going on? There are some men outside carrying guns!'

'Have Jarvis escort you down to the hotel. Wait there for me.'

She searched the men's faces and then nodded. 'All right, Hilly. Whatever you say.'

'Better not.' Slone drew his gun, suddenly taking charge. He nodded to Lovendaul. 'Keep her and the boss man covered, Zip.'

'What's the meaning of this, Slone?' Hilton was incredulous. 'You don't give me orders in my own house!'

'Your house,' he grunted with disgust. 'It was always about you . . . you and that featherbrained wife of yours!'

Hilton took a step towards him, fists raised, his face red with an immediate fury. 'No one talks about Flora that way!'

Slone cocked his gun. 'One more step. . . .'

Flora grabbed hold of Hilton's arm. 'No! Hilly!' she cried. 'Do what they say!'

'I got a wire this morning, from the same railroad people Nodean visited. There's no proposed spur coming this way. If you want to run rail for about a hundred miles, they might let us ship coal on their railroad.' He snorted his contempt. 'All of our time and money has been spent so you could play the rich man, woo the big shots from the railroad and run a spur for our coal mine. Well, it ain't going to happen! It's over!'

'We can swing a loan, hire the men and lay track ourselves.' Hilton was desperate. 'There has to be a way!'

'Maybe in ten years, when the demand for coal increases enough to make the railroad come this way.

Until then, we're throwing good money after bad. That's all finished now.'

'What are you going to do?'

'I want all the money from your safe. Me and the boys are going to get out of this little fix, and you two are going to help us!'

Yancy held his rifle at the ready position. His shoulder and left side was on fire. It was all he could do to fight down the pain. He was in the back of the wagon with Wade and John. Konrad and Chaw were to either side, both ready for a fight.

'Hello the house!' Konrad's booming voice called out. 'This is US Marshal Ellington. I want all of you to come out with your hands clear of any weapon. We want no shooting here today.'

'What do you want?' Queen called from an open window. 'What's a US Marshal doing in Pine Junction?'

'I'm here to oversee the election and speak to your local law enforcement. There's no cause for alarm.'

'Yeah?' Queen sneered. 'So why bring a half-dozen men with guns?'

'Come on out, boys. We don't want anyone hurt or killed.'

Slone appeared at the door. 'You and your men hold your fire, Marshal. We're coming out!'

But it wasn't Slone or one of his deputies to come out first. Flora was in the lead and Slone had a gun pointed at her back. Queen followed with a gun on Hilton, while Lovendaul was on the other side, his gun pointed out towards the small posse.

'You can have Hilton Conway, Marshal,' Slone spoke up. 'But we're going to take the lady with us for a short way. Once we have a good head-start, we'll let her go.'

'No!' Hilton shouted, trying to reach Flora. 'I won't allow—'

Queen bounced his gun muzzle in a glancing blow off of Hilton's skull to silence his objection. He staggered down the front steps and sank to his knees.

Flora cried out in alarm and tried to run to him. Her reaction surprised Slone. He was twisted about, forced to reach out and catch hold of her by the hair. However, due to her movement and straining against him, his gun was no longer pointing at her.

Yancy had a split-second. The man was clear in his sights. He pulled the trigger.

Stone was spun about from the impact of a bullet tearing high into his gun arm. The pistol flew from his hand.

Konrad had his own gun out. 'Hold it!' he shouted the warning.

Lovendaul fired wildly at them, his bullet thudding into the side of the wagon. It was the only shot he got off. Konrad returned fire and a slug tore through his chest and knocked him over backwards.

Queen dropped his gun and threw his hands into the air. 'Don't shoot!' he wailed. 'Don't shoot!'

Chaw had the man under his own gun. He uttered a grunt of disgust. 'I knew you didn't have the guts for a fight, Queen.'

'Hilly!' Flora was on her knees, examining the bump on the man's head. 'I'm so sorry, Hilly.'

Hilton was still dazed, but he looked up at his wife. The love and devotion shone in his face. 'Now, now, Flora, honey,' he soothed. 'You've nothing to be sorry for. I'm the one who is sorry.'

'No, Hilly.' She was resolute. 'You were mayor of Pine Junction. You did everything you could to win the railroad spur. I know you did it all for me.'

Hilton gave his head a shake. 'Flora, honey, I needed the money it would have provided. With the railroad, I could have bought you the world.'

She looked over at the wounded Slone, then at Lovendaul's lifeless body. 'You've been wrong about me, Hilly,' she said quietly. 'I was born in the slums of New York.' Her voice was as soft as a baby's whisper. 'My unwed mother left me on the doorstep of a church. In all of my childhood I was hungry, ragged and cold. I swore that nothing would keep me from getting everything money could buy, but. . . .' Her voice broke, tears sliding down her cheeks. 'But this is too much. You've been so good to me, Hilly.'

'Flora, honey, I. . . .'

She shook her head negatively. 'I have put my own needs before everything else. I wanted to have it all. I wanted to be a lady, to be respected and envied. But I never wanted to hurt anyone.'

'You've done nothing to anyone.' Hilton defended her quickly.

She looked at him and smiled. 'I think I might actually love you, Hilly. You've been so perfect, tried so hard to do everything in the world for me. . . .'

'I wanted to make you happy.'

'We'll face this together,' she promised him. 'No matter what the court says, we'll see it through.'

'Whatever you say, Flora, honey.'

'And if you go to prison, I'll wait for you.'

Slone, still holding his injured arm, spat into the dusty street. 'Dad blame! I was right! She is a featherbrain!'

'I gave the orders to Slone!' Hilton spoke to Konrad. 'I levied the taxes and used the money to try and persuade the railroad people to run a line up here. However, I never ordered anyone beaten or hurt and I never told anyone to set fire to Cal's tavern. That's the truth, Marshal.'

Konrad gave a nod of his head, but looked over at Yancy. 'Looks like your pardon is going through, Nodean. You've brought peace to Pine Junction, just like I asked.'

'And Chaw Benedict?'

'He still has to do his time,' he said with a grin. 'Another year as city marshal ought to about settle his score. I'll send along his pardon too.'

Few people in town attended the funeral for Zip Lovendaul. He didn't have any friends. As for the misuse of city funds, Hilton was sentenced to one year in prison. Slone was given ten years and Queen got two. True to his word, both Chaw and Yancy received a letter saying their records were clean.

As for Hilton's house, belongings and money, it was sold or returned to the city treasury. Chaw hired the banker to determine how much of a refund each person would receive.

Yancy was there to see Flora off.

'That really was a lovely saddle you made for me, Mr Nodean,' she said, before climbing aboard the stage. 'I should like for you to have it back. Perhaps your daughter or your lady friend will decide to ride and enjoy sitting a horse like a proper lady.'

'Thank you.'

Allyson came to stand at Yancy's side. She asked: 'What will you do?'

Flora sighed. 'I'm going to rent a place in the town nearest the territorial prison. From there, I can visit Hilton, write letters to him, and await his release.'

'How will you live?'

'They let me keep my jewelry. I can sell it for enough to live off for the year and still have a little for when Hilton gets out.' She laughed. 'Who knows? We might start our own little business somewhere.'

'I wish you both luck, Mrs Conway,' Yancy said. Then with a loving glance at Allyson, 'I know how far a man will go for the love of a woman.'

She stepped up into the waiting stagecoach. After closing the door, she smiled at them through the window. 'I wish you luck too, Mr Nodean . . . you and your family.'

He backed away from the stage and waved. The lady was still as pretty as if she had stepped out of a painting.

'Flora must be about the most beautiful woman in the world,' Allyson said, wistfully, obviously thinking along the same lines.

'Yep,' Yancy teased. 'I reckon she is about the most beautiful woman in the world.'

The statement brought the thread of a frown to Allyson's expression. It was the desired reaction he sought. 'Next to you, that is.'

That also worked as planned. Allyson flushed from the compliment, then snuggled close and kissed him. He wondered if maybe he might yet figure out women.

'Kara is waiting for us,' Allyson said. 'She has taught Bunny a new trick. You are going to love it.'

'Oh?'

'She throws your shoe and Bunny brings it back. Then they have a tug-of-war over it.' She laughed lightly. 'Your boots aren't going to last very long.'

He let out a deep sigh. 'Tough being a family man.'

'Not as tough as being alone.'

Yancy put his arm around her shoulders and started for their house. 'No, not as tough as being alone, and I don't intend to be alone again. I think I'll keep you around . . . even after you finish your full sixty days of servitude.'

'Is that supposed to be a proposal of marriage?'

He shrugged his shoulder. 'I'm not a very forthright man.'

'You really do need me. I'd better stay around and help you for a little while – say the rest of our lives.'

'Sounds great to me,' he grinned, holding her closer. 'Yep, it sounds great to me.'